A Chance to See Egypt

Sandra Scofield

The death of Tom Riley's wife left him "tilting, out of balance." He travels to Mexico, where they honeymooned, as a pilgrimage to love's memory. An American writer, herself an expatriate escaping from her painful past, befriends him, sensing that he has a story to tell. "Change the plot," she advises. "Introduce new characters."

Enter a Mexican woman and her daughter, who defy the stereotypes of the passive peasant. Strong willed and mystical, Consolata Arispe runs a small cafe and plans her children's survival. Divina—the most beautiful girl in town—dreams of white houses and sings American songs. Their mystery and beauty enchant Riley and draw him into the life of their village. There, fates converge, secrets are revealed, and open hearts are filled.

A fanciful tale of love's charms and an illustration of the mystical in an ordinary man, *A Chance to See Egypt* is a novel that proves that the story we choose to tell is the life we choose to live.

Also by Sandra Scofield

Opal on Dry Ground
More Than Allies
Walking Dunes
Beyond Deserving
Gringa

A
CHANCE
TO
SEE
EGYPT

Sandra Scofield

Cliff Street Books

An Imprint of HarperPerennial
A Division of HarperCollins*Publishers*

A hardcover edition of this book was published in 1996 by HarperCollins Publishers.

HarperCollins books may be purchased for educational, business, or sales promotional use. For information please write: Special Markets Department, HarperCollins Publishers, Inc., 10 East 53rd Street, New York, NY 10022.

First Cliff Street Books/HarperPerennial edition published 1997.

Designed by C. Linda Dingler

The Library of Congress has catalogued the hardcover edition as follows:

Scofield, Sandra Jean
   A chance to see Egypt : a novel / Sandra Scofield.
      p.   cm.
   ISBN 0-06-017343-2
   1. Americans—Travel—Mexico—Fiction. 2. Mothers and daughters—Mexico—Fiction. 3. Women authors—Mexico—Fiction. 4. Villages—Mexico—Fiction.
I. Title.
PS3569.C584C48   1996
813' .54—dc20   95-51834

ISBN 0-06-092788-7 (pbk.)

97 98 99 00 01 ❖/RRD 10 9 8 7 6 5 4 3 2 1

For Patty and Vince
and for Bill

The merry may eat of the fruit,
The weeping are stabbed with the thorns.

MEXICAN FOLK SONG

I know the existence of God.
What with, is the question.

ANNE TRUITT, DAYBOOK

Contents

PART TWO
In Which a Man Finds a Bed in a
Dusty Village,
New Friendships Are Forged,
and Passion Is Ignited

PART THREE
In Which a Soul Is Tormented,
a Painting Unveiled,
and a New Tale Begins

PART ONE

In Which a Man Makes a Pilgrimage,
an Artist Hides from Her Shadows,
and a Mother Burns Herbs

A
Circus

MR. RILEY CAME TO LAGO DE LUZ TO GRIEVE.

That is the beginning.

But there you have the notion of a sad man, and I won't tell you a sad story. This is a tale of love's charms and lovers' follies, of a girl who dreams of houses, and a man who travels alone.

Start instead at the end. Start with a circus. We will find our way there again.

It is a mile from the highway to the Street of Three Saddles, which runs like a border along the edge of the village of Tecatitlán. Across the flat floor of the valley road, early one spring morning, trucks and tractor-trailers and vans came chugging and lumbering in a long, colorful caravan. Villagers, hearing the rumble, streamed to the Street of Three Saddles. They spread out like a ribbon and stood transfixed, watching the circus entourage heave into a circle on a field of stunted grasses, there to set up camp. Later that morning, a dilapidated yellow Dodge cruised the plaza, its loudspeaker blaring news of a six o'clock show. Later still a band of schoolchildren straggled about town, playing rude flutes and tin drums, bearing a banner that read: LIVE ANIMALS! DARING FEATS!

A circus in Tecatitlán! Is this a stop between larger venues? Or a kind of gift? (At five pesos a person, and only one for a child, they won't break even.) Is it an accident of events, converging because sometimes in the life of a village more than one wonderful thing can happen on the same day?

Or does it simply make a good story?

It is a day the children will not forget, the day they rode an elephant. Six at a time on the back of the beast, the children cling to one another, their eyes wide with delight and terror, while the tuxedoed handler leads them around in a circle in the sawdust.

A day the young acrobat Magdalena won't forget, when the seam of her bodice split and one heavy breast burst free.

A day the young man (always a boy) the village calls Poor One won't forget, when he sits all day at the cage of the two tired tigers, his ear filled with the grumble of their bellies, their hot sighs, their hisses, and finally, frightfully, wonderfully, their roars.

And Thomas Riley, a man out of place, between the two humps of a camel like a coin in a slot, waves blindly into the lights, a man giving, and receiving, blessing.

At the
Posada Celestial

From his room at the Posada Celestial, Mr. Riley can see the gardens and the mineral pool. In the morning, he hears the maids chattering in the hall and, through the high open window of the kitchen below his room, the cook bantering with the help. When he arrived and asked for a room on the inner court, the pretty young receptionist tried to put him on the street side, with its view (barely) of the lake, or at the back, away from the kitchen. But he remembers the room happily, and he has come for the purpose of indulging in reverie. He likes waking to the sounds of young voices, remembering where he is and how the water of the lake stretches away like a milky sea.

You would not call the Posada Celestial a resort, although ninety years ago it was a home away from home for Don Porfirio. It is a small hotel in a small town. Lago de Luz, on the *altiplano* far from the sea, where it is neither hot nor cold, boasts no buildings higher than two stories, and no slick discos. It is rather a sleepy place, swollen on weekends when musicians and vendors make the plaza festive for the tourists in from the nearby city. Resident Americans and Canadians make their own social life in their suburban enclaves and trailer parks, their apartments and houses, halls and meeting rooms. The Lakeside Society is the hub of activity, the place where everyone crosses, but there are many diversions: Elk Clubs, Rotarians, Veterans Clubs, Red Cross, and all the interest groups, for cards and dominoes and self-improvement. At the Celestial, guests come in pairs, like aging passengers on an ark. They float above their lives, where there is nothing they must do.

The Celestial, sitting flush on the promenade, a short walk from the pier, is a brief stopover for tour buses. Mr. and Mrs. Riley first came this way off such a bus, through the lobby and dining room, onto the long cool back veranda where tables were laid with bowls of punch and platters of sliced papayas. They were met by a band of winter residents not yet committed to property, who offered bits of information indulgently, like truffles. "We bathe in the sulfur pool before bed," they said. "We eat fruit from the trees on the grounds behind the hotel."

They could see shadows lapping, lake-like, on the stones of the deep veranda. Along the edges were hibiscus and oleanders, and flowerpots of geraniums. The perfume of orange trees wafted in the air like a cloud. As evening fell, guests wandered inside for frosty margaritas. They went on to tell tales that went with the town and the hotel, in the manner of village pundits. As if there were wisdom in remembering the bandits of another era, the old sailing boats and canoes, the movie stars, the whitefish, splendid when the lake was clean.

"We'll come back," the Rileys said. They meant another year, but there are many cities and villages, in many countries, in all parts of the world, and there were so many they wished to see. They talked of Egypt. They were eager for the exotic.

Mrs. Riley was interested in shrines and apparitions, tales of martyrs and miracles, but these were not the people to ask. She whispered to her husband that they would rent a car. They would find the byways. She was resourceful and eager and experienced; it amused her to appear grateful for bare news of other hot springs, the Indian village of Tecatitlán, the house of a famous writer, long dead. So it was they decided to rearrange their itinerary, to skip the birds in the mangrove swamp on the coast, and the idle pleasures of a washed-white resort. They took the room above the kitchen, or, actually, a suite of two rooms and a large bath at the corner. They settled in. They visited the beautiful railway station, and strolled the promenade to the edge of the lake where boats bobbed on a surface of water hyacinths. They liked the nearby Indian village better, and walked its every street. They rented a car, and ventured out and up, to mountain towns. It was their honeymoon. They took a hundred pictures, as if they could forget.

A
Change of Direction

I STUDIED PAINTING AT A FAMOUS SCHOOL IN PHILADELPHIA. When I was nineteen, after a competition, they gave me my own studio. It had a skylight. Most days I kept the door wide open, like the other students. Someone would play the radio. Once in a while we called out to one another. After a few hours, we were quiet. We forgot about one another, the door, the music. There was just the light and our work. In this way, I would have two years to act like an artist before I went out to try to live like one. I didn't worry about money yet. With the studio, there was a scholarship. My mother sent a small check every month. I lived with other students, ate noodles, slept on a mattress on the floor.

Toward the end of the first year I met a man in the European Paintings gallery of the Metropolitan Museum of Art in New York. We were both admiring a Bellini Madonna. I should have guessed. He was a man looking for an aesthetic wife. I was tired of standing alone in a room wondering with

every brushstroke, Will I ever be good enough? Charlotte
Amory, successful student, was one person; Charlotte
Amory, artist, was someone else entirely.

I don't intend to tell the story of my life. Only the barest
bit is relevant to the tale I do want to tell. Beginning with
the Madonna and Child. I abandoned my art training, married the man from the gallery, and moved to Rye. I learned to
cook. I had a child, Phoebe, and the year she was three, in
stolen hours and hidden crannies, I wrote a novel. I wanted
to paint, but I had little space, I couldn't leave a still life set
up, the light was bad. Words were easier. I sent the novel in
over the transom (this was possible twenty years ago), and in
short order my book was everywhere. For a little while, I
was famous.

I see us standing before the Bellini. I remember noticing him
out of the corner of my eye, and then he was closer, leaning
forward a little to examine the painting, "accidentally" brushing my arm. I said something art-schoolish. Perhaps I commented on the red curtain cutting the background asymmet-
rically, something like, "He was very daring for his time."
Implying that I was for mine, a Texas girl in a Manhattan
museum. So far from Wimberly.

The novel was called *She Would.*

Each chapter was titled. For example:
"She Would Find Meaning in Art."
"She Would Live a Bohemian Life."

(In the novel, the protagonist had a walkup in the Village. She was plucked from her blossoming career by an art
collector and seduced by promises of having it all.)

"She Would Bear His Child."

And so on, until: "She Would Die a Domestic Death," in
which she attempted suicide.

And then, of course, "She Would Begin Again."

It was one of half a dozen "mad-housewife" novels of the early seventies. Rambling, self-indulgent, intimate, and—I have to remind myself now—fresh for its time. I was tenth on the *New York Times* bestseller list for two weeks. I traveled for six weeks giving readings. In bookstores, people asked me if I drew on my own life, if I wrote in longhand, if I felt my life had changed. Yes, yes, I said. Oh yes.

When I returned home I felt like a stranger. I felt in danger of suffocation, like the protagonist of my novel. I had made a terrible mistake, but I could fix it. I was young. I could start over.

So there is the obligatory scene: My daughter at five. Me, trying to explain. *Mommy has to go.*

My words, my face, my pain. Her father was steely. He said, Phoebe is not negotiable.

My daughter's face soft-focus, her cries soundless.

In my book the child was annoyingly precocious, obviously allied with her father. A child you could abandon.

I think instead of the red curtain in the Bellini painting. How I wondered what was behind it, how I felt lured by the slice of autumn landscape in the left quadrant of the picture. How I might have said, *Excuse me,* and moved on.

Of course I tried to write another novel. Novels.

Every couple of years I began a new one. I told myself I needed more gestation time, but I knew what my problem was. I didn't have any ideas, not ones big enough for books. There was nothing for which I cared enough to make a novel. I was dry. And I had to make a living. I had walked away from everything. My mother, who owned a small motel and a gift shop in tiny Wimberly, near San Marcos, in the Texas hill country, didn't speak to me for years. I had "thrown away" the education she had struggled to provide and then, when she was happy that I had a family, I had thrown that away, too. My father made no judgments about those things—he didn't have much invested in me, to tell the truth—and he tried to give me a little help now and then, but he was never good with his own money, and he got tired. He was a drug salesman, always on the road, going in the back doors of doctors' offices and hospitals. At sixty, he married again, a woman with kids, and more than had his hands full and his pockets empty. I really was on my own at last.

I was invited now and then to a writers' conference, and I caught on to the concept of workshops. I started offering the very thing I needed myself—exercises that dug at story. "Start with your childhood stories," I said. "Tell them from the point of view of your siblings, your cousins. Write the stories you tell strangers on airplanes. The stories your family told that taught you your charter of beliefs. Tell the stories you are afraid to tell. The ones the culture needs to hear. Don't be afraid of the shadow side: shame, despair, the dirty little secrets."

I was lucky. I hit the time when legions were hungry for meaning and had the money to pursue it. I wrote a new book, this one on writing. It was called *False Starts and True Beginnings*, and though it was a slow starter, it ultimately sold more than the novel, and still sells today. The trickle of royalties has been like an annuity, and the reputation got me work on a circuit of college campuses. And nobody called my bluff.

Until I got sick of hearing myself tell other people to do what I had never been able to do: tell the truth, even if it is fiction. I knew these things, but I couldn't do anything about it.

I came here thinking I could eke out an existence for the better part of a year, that I would finally write something solid. If not, I told myself, I would get vocational training, as a respiratory therapist, maybe; there are always people with bad lungs. The surprise is, I'm still here. I haven't written anything I can show the world, except for a few off-the-beaten-path travel articles, but I work at it every day. It's like a Guggenheim fellowship six times over, only Guggenheim fellows don't sleep with their landlords.

A
New Face

MY WRITING CLASS AT THE LAKESIDE SOCIETY LIBRARY had been meeting once a week for several months when Tom Riley showed up for the first time. He had just arrived in Lago de Luz the day before. He saw my poster in the hotel lobby, he said, next to one that read *Moonlight Meditation*. He had no particular plans; he had no traveling companions. Why not a class?

The other participants welcomed him warmly. There were eleven of them—five Canadians, the rest from the U.S., mostly from the cold upper Midwest states. They were a comfortable group. We had progressed beyond the ingenuously charming and the baldly sentimental. They were no longer shy with one another, and the women had stopped deferring to the men. They ranged in age from their early sixties to seventy-five or so. It was no small thing to nudge the women beyond exclamations of, "Oh, I couldn't read it out loud!"

They had begun to speak of "the writer's craft."

I have been teaching writing, off and on, for nearly twenty years, and I know what it means when students ask for criticism. If they are "serious about writing"—say students in a college evening class or a summer workshop, for which they have traveled and paid plenty—they mean they want you to tell them what to "fix" so they can send their manuscript off to your agent and the agent can sell their work and they can become much better known than you. If they are, like these folks, writing because their lives have become pure leisure in need of filling, they want to be appreciated, plain and simple. They want you to love them.

In the days when I made my way from campus to campus, I developed a neutral posture that sometimes frustrated students but seemed, in the end, fairest. I had learned that I could not evaluate the beginning writer's prospects with any significant accuracy, for talent was often not the primary factor in future success. I could not know—indeed, the students often did not know—who would give his life over to it. And that is what it takes. So I tried to set them up to discover what they had to learn. No one could accuse me of discouragement, just as no one went away clutching my praise and false promise. My job, I always said, was to make them independent. They had to be their own best critics.

Now that my teaching is on a par with the golf pro's and the potter's—we are all keeping ourselves afloat as if Lago de Luz were a cruise ship—I operate very differently. I try earnestly to guide these retirees toward whatever gives them pleasure. They want to remember their parents and their childhoods. They want to recall the antics of their own children. And, as the palate craves pepper, they want to feel the bite of memory, too; they want to remind themselves—and one another—that they have survived.

*   *   *

At first, I was nervous about a new person. Would he upset the intimacy of the group? Would I have to coddle him? As the group poured their coffee and settled at the tables, I thought about changing the topic back to something blander. Then I realized I was thinking of this Mr. Riley as an old man, and that he was not. He appeared to be in his mid-forties, a mild, good-looking man, flat in the belly and butt, with most of his hair, and a shy, chin-tucked, unassuming manner. He had a slightly rumpled, pleasant look, his features charmingly crooked, his smile boyish. I thought right away that I might like him. I relaxed, and went on with my plans.

The assignment was to remember a betrayal. As always, it was met with a hush and a rustle, then an array of earnest, scrunched-up faces as my writers pondered the task. In a few moments, they were all bent over their pads and the only sounds were the scratches of their pens and the calls of birds in the lovely garden just outside. Only Mr. Riley, new student that he was, chewed on his pencil, slow to make the leap to some first thought.

"Wait, Mr. Riley," I said when the class broke up. "Are you in a hurry?"

I could see he was surprised. I suggested we walk toward the plaza. He said, "Do you know a place where I can get a good *torta*? I remember liking them a lot." I liked them too—a version of the sandwich, on crusty rolls.

I took him to my favorite lunch place, the Patio. The owner, Consolata Arispe, greeted me as always, as one dear and seldom seen, although that very morning I had waved to her as she stood on the side of the road waiting for the rickety bus from Tecatitlán. She rushed to bring us a napkin-lined basket of tortilla chips, hot from her pan.

Her black hair was drawn back in a tight braid, and she wore silver hoops for earrings. Like most of the village women, she was short, but she always carried herself—even in the bustle of her work—with such assurance and poise, I often found myself thinking what a lovely woman she was.

Neither Riley nor I was ready for lunch. We decided to have fruit drinks, the sort of thing we call smoothies in the states, and save the *tortas* for another time soon.

He said I should call him Riley—everyone did, though his name was Thomas. I, after all, had introduced myself as "Charlotte Amory, call me Charlotte." After that was out of the way, I decided to say what was on my mind.

"You are much too young to be in my group," I said.

This distressed him. "I'm sorry." His crinkled eyes were the picture of worry.

Of course I hadn't meant there was an age requirement. It was only an observation. "Retirees are usually much older."

"I'm not retired. I'm only here for a little while." He ran a finger up and down his glass. He didn't look at me as he said, "I didn't know where else to go."

I gasped, and tried to disguise it with a cough. What he said—I had said the very same thing myself, if not the exact words, years ago, when I first came to the lake. I had been speaking to a smoothly handsome Mexican man, albeit in the cool darkness of a hotel bar, and I had known as soon as I said it that I wasn't going to leave if I didn't have to.

"Oh, Tom Riley," I said. I really could not help myself. "Don't you know people come here at the end of their lives?"

He said, "Don't you know lives can be over a long time before you die?"

He had a story, and I wanted to know it. I lifted my banana-strawberry-orange concoction in a salute. "Life is just a tale you're telling. Change the plotline. Introduce new characters," I told him.

I had done neither for a long time.

The
Great House

FOUR YEARS AGO, I moved into my room at the Great House. I brought with me a suitcase full of books on writing. Some were heady academic tomes on the nature of narrative and myth. Some were old college textbooks. Some were classics on writing fiction. Every night, sometime after dark, I sat down at a table and I worked. I wasn't trying to write anything to sell; no one would ever see these exercises. I was trying to learn my craft. I told myself not to hurry. A few months ago, I began to construct my little sketches of the village.

I don't pretend to know these people, to know the depth or breadth of their sorrows, to know who is wise and who is foolish. Who knows anyone? It's all a lesson—writing is—in empathy. And arrogance. I use them, as writers do, making what I can of what I see and what I surmise, choosing them as subject because they are here—because I am here—and because I sense something in their lives that I would like to understand. Being grateful for their gift—what Henry James called the *donnée*. The things that happen, the things I see. I think that in this way I would build, not just my craft, but my salvation.

I go to bed late, maybe two in the morning, sometimes later. I sleep until midmorning unless I am teaching a class, and even then I would never set the time earlier than ten-thirty. I like to go out for a little while each day to see the life of the village and then again at night to sit in the courtyard by the chapel. There is my mail to fetch. I often drive over to Lago de Luz and eat lunch there. I sometimes spend a few hours at the Lakeside Society Library. Every few weeks I go to some outlying village or town. Lately, I have been sketching on these forays. There is always something to do.

In the afternoons I draw or paint. At first I was over-whelmed with despair. It had been many years since I had tried to render anything, and my drawing skills had disap-peared. But I had time. I just kept at it. I practiced in what I thought was the secrecy of my rooms at the Great House, though I should have realized that anything I did, seen by the maid, would become common knowledge. At first I arranged still life setups on tables or on the ledge of the win-dow in my room, or outside on the veranda or in the court-yard. Then I began drawing parts of the buildings them-selves: the marvelous stones and carved doors, the gargoyles and the statues of saints. I spent a week once sketching the landlord's old white hairless dog Loza. Eventually I went into Guadalajara and bought everything I needed to begin paint-ing again, at first in watercolor. After a while, I did a small painting in oils of a bowl of fruit, a tablet, and a straw hat. There was something stunning, almost holy, about color coming from my brushes, like sight after blindness. The rib-bon on the hat was vermilion.

Late one afternoon nearly a year after I had come to live

in the village, I was putting everything away when the maid came and stood behind me until I felt her presence and asked what it was. She said there was a girl from the village who wished to see me. "I will send her away if you say," she said. The maid, Sofia, was only fifteen, but she had worked at the Great House since she was eleven, before I came, and she had a certain status in the village that gave her some authority with shopkeepers and vendors, repairmen and the like, rather as if she were a housekeeper in a hotel. This was especially true now that her young cousin Nola had come to work—Nola could not have been more than ten years old. I sensed that Sofia felt disdain for my caller, and it made me curious.

"No, send her in," I said. "I am done here. And you may go."

"I have not set out your supper."

"There is enough in the kitchen. I will do it myself. Really, give yourself an hour." I smiled, knowing Sofia's vanity. "Enough time to wash your hair," I suggested. At Christmas I had given her shampoo that smelled of apples.

She was impassive, unreadable. I had offended her. "At your orders," she said. In a moment she returned with another girl about her own age. She walked slightly behind the girl, and I had the impression she meant to push her toward me. I stepped toward them and bade Sofia good night. I felt the sharpness of my dismissal, though, and the presumptuousness of my familiarity. The only way I knew to smooth it over was to act within the boundaries of our roles where, oddly, I often felt uneasy and she was the strong one. I asked her to pick up oranges for me in the morning on her way to work and to bring me my coffee at nine. She nodded curtly and turned with a toss of her head so that her long ponytail swung.

The visitor was a girl I had probably seen about the vil-

lage but had not really observed, or I would have noticed
how beautiful she was. She was almost my height, in a place
where few of the villagers were more than five feet tall. Her
glossy black hair fell in two plump braids over her breasts and
hung to her waist. She had Indian features—the broad planes
of her cheeks, the elegant bridge of her nose—but because
she had a longer, narrower face than most, these features
looked entirely different on her. Her eyelashes were lustrous,
her eyebrows dark slashes above, and her eyes were astonish-
ing, for they were not the expected dark brown. Rather, her
eyes were a flecked hazel color, like rare stones. And her
skin—she was obviously of mixed ancestry—seemed to glow,
burnished at the cheeks. I could not tell much about her figure, since she was dressed in a full skirt and had a shawl
wrapped around her head and shoulders, but she stood with
a graceful, modest, but unintimidated posture.

She quite took my breath away.

"I have come for work," she said.

"I don't think—"

"Only a little work. I have a job in Lago, but I want more
to do. There are some things I wish to buy."

"But I have Sofia," I protested. I didn't want to send her
away, though.

"I have worked for an American family in Lago," she said.
"I have run the machines in the house and cared for babies."

I smiled. "There are no babies here."

She was undeterred. "I can embroider and mend. I read.
I write a little." Then, surprisingly, she switched to English
for a moment. "I speak a little English and I wish to learn
more." She raised her hand to her mouth and lowered her
head. I wasn't sure I believed her embarrassment, but she
did go back to Spanish.

"My mother has taught me to rub oils and herbs to
soothe your aches. And I know herbs for teas."

My God, I thought, *she's going to go on forever. Whatever can she want so much?*

I asked her.

"I want music tapes, and a machine to play them. And I want to practice English with a gringo."

"But that's not so much!" I was immensely relieved. The thought had flashed through my mind that she might be pregnant, that there might be something she expected me, the gringa, to do about that. This was nothing. I had a boombox I never used; I could give it to her.

"I don't need any of these things," I said quietly. I saw disappointment in her eyes, but she did not move. "Sofia's cousin Nola comes to the house now, and there is the gardener. Surely you can save a little each week from your Lago job—"

I could have bitten my tongue out at the condescension. I knew how little these children were paid, how meager their lives were, but there was some perverse impulse in me to test her mettle. I knew I did not want one more petulant peasant in my life—a thought of which I was ashamed, and which I would never have spoken to anyone.

She bowed her head, raised it, and turned without speaking, all with the languor and grace of a moment in film. I watched her take a few steps, then knew I could not bear to let her go. "Wait!" I cried.

She turned. Her chin quivered.

"There is something—not much, I tell you. But you could earn a radio. You could do that. I could use a model. I would like to draw you. You would sit for me." I gestured toward my things.

She stared at me for a moment and then, as if it were something she had done many times before, she let her shawl slide down around her shoulders into a lovely drape. She smiled. She had good white teeth. I felt like someone seduced by an animal. I felt inspired and compelled.

"Come on Wednesday," I said. "When are you free in the afternoon?"

"I return to the village at one-thirty. Sometimes a little later."

"Come at three. For two hours." I named a sum. It was very little. If she was good, I would give her more, but I did not want to build up too much hope, for either of us.

"I am called Divina Arispe," she said. "And you are Charlotte Amory."

"Divina." I had to suppress my happy laugh. "Of course you are."

So we began what has become three years of collaboration and companionship. A gringa painter and a peasant model. Picasso would eat his heart out.

A
Frequent Flyer

WHEN RILEY HAD ANNOUNCED HIS PLANS, his sister Margaret had said, "You can't run from sorrow, Tom," in a way that seemed sympathetic—the sound of it, the sad expression on her face—but struck him as meddling. Come to think of it, Margaret had always meddled, and he had always brushed her advice and inquiries and arrangements aside gently, as the efforts of a fussy woman who loved him and meant well. This time, though, he felt stubbornness stiffen his spine. "I can cry in some warmer place, at least," he said.

It was funny to think he was using award checks from an airline to make the trip. He did not think of himself as a frequent flyer, but in the eight years of his marriage, he had accompanied Eva to meetings and resorts all over the United States. He had toured New England when the leaves fell, and the Southwest when the Indians danced. He had bicycled in North Carolina, and floated down a calm green river in Texas. Sometimes he didn't know what they were going to be doing until they arrived. Eva made all the decisions and arrangements. Travel was her business. They came back from their honeymoon excited about more trips to other countries. They perused hundreds of brochures as time passed, but somehow another foreign trip never happened.

Eva was occupied with her specialty tours—pilgrimages to sacred sites and shrines—and there never seemed to be an itinerary right for the two of them. She was sorry, she said; there would be time later. She went without him. To Delphi for the autumn solstice. To Benares and the Taj Majal. To Lourdes and Fatima, Assisi, Rome. The stone hillsides of Iona in the Hebrides. A shrine of the Black Madonna in Sicily.

He was busy with the store and church affairs. He cheered when his sister Margaret accompanied Eva to visit Mary cathedrals throughout France. He was happy to see a rodeo in Wyoming, a music festival in the Berkshires. He was happy to read about Egypt.

Early that last winter, seeing him stretched out in bed reading *The Rape of the Nile,* Eva had suggested they go to Egypt for their tenth anniversary. That would give them time to plan and study. Maybe a little Arabic.

Right after that, they saw a documentary on the public TV station about the artisans who documented life on the walls of the tombs. They lived in villages together. This was their life's work; it seemed noble to Riley. He imagined himself writing on the walls of his house. He would draw a long banquet table, and seat his mother, his sister and her family, Eva and her slow, sweet daughter Bernadette. His friends at church and families from the neighborhood. The animals, in special high chairs.

Margaret was appalled that he intended to revisit the town where he had been so happy with Eva. "Why go there without her?" she said. "What would she think?"

He had no idea what his dear wife would say. She had been a woman of strong opinions, who stood tall and moved briskly, and he had happily followed her lead in everything from remodeling the house to setting the dinner hour, but they had not considered the possibility of his being widowed. They had not foreseen the vast emptiness of life alone, the numbness of spirit, the absence of will. She had been dead a year and a half, and he still felt like a man on a tilting floor swaying for balance.

He needed to do something. He wanted his memories to be flowers, not torturous nettles. If his only joys were to be past ones, he would try to celebrate them. He wanted to make his life a shrine to love; only he would know of it; only he would be its pilgrim.

Until he met Eva, he had lived a life so uneventful, so without particulars, it might have been ordered from a catalog. Eva had come after he had stopped thinking he would have a life companion. She had been widowed by the Vietnam War when she was little more than a girl. He expressed surprise that she had been alone so long. She had been waiting to see what her special child Bernadette would grow up to do. She said no one before him had been suitable. Of course, for him, Bernadette had been no test; she had already become independent. The girl liked him; he liked her. Eva said Bernadette was never wrong about people; it was a kind of gift, to balance her handicap.

Eva swelled his worth, then poked and prodded him to live up to it. He studied to improve his Spanish, learned to race-walk, read writers he had once thought too intellectual (Proust, Márquez, Kazantzakis, Greene). He wanted then to be the man Eva had seen in him; he wanted to be that man now. And what he did was entirely his own business. A dazzling thought.

*   *   *

The night before he left, he got out the slide projector and the honeymoon slides. Of course the bulb was burned out, and he had to go out in falling snow to buy a new one. He came back chilled and eager. He screwed the bulb in and clicked the carousel into motion. It was loaded just as it was the day Eva died. He had not had the courage to look again until now, but the motions of propping the carousel up, pulling his chair around to a proper spot, and the weight of the clicker in his hand—all these things busied him. He had read that someday in the not too far distant future, you would be able to phone people and see them on a screen. Maybe that would feel a little like this. For the moments she was projected on the white wall, Eva was not entirely gone. She smiled at him from her pose beside the dry fountain in the Indian village. Sunlight struck her face and washed out the details of her features. She had not tried to shade her eyes with her hand. She held her arms out from her body like a dancer. Though she was tall and sturdy, she looked light, like someone about to float. To ascend.

Simple
Devotion

THIS WAS RILEY'S FIRST TRIP ALONE. Until he married Eva, he had only been out of Chicago three times, each time in the company of others. When he was a boy, his mother took him and his sister on the bus—she had never learned to drive—to see Lincoln's birthplace. He remembers nothing of the trip except the bus, nothing of museums or plaques or where they spent the night. He sat across the aisle from his sister and mother, beside a man who smelled of cigarettes and licorice.

The second venture was his senior class trip to Philadelphia, where he saw the Liberty Bell and Betsy Ross's house. The students slept on the bus and survived on hot dogs and candy. He was a jumble of emotions. He longed to sit beside a girl named Carrie Tucker. She was sweet and smart, with dark braids and crackling escaped hairs around her face. She was shy like him, but, though he agonized and rehearsed what to say, imagining the touch of her skirted thigh, he never got up the nerve to speak to her. On the way back she sat with another boy. She slept with her head on that braver boy's shoulder.

When he was almost thirty, he went away with some young men from the Knights of Columbus group to a monastery in Arkansas for a week's retreat. He fell in love with the rolling hills, the cool old stone buildings, the quiet beauty of the grounds. There was an air of gentle rectitude and simple devotion. He had a sense of being at home. He could imagine himself working in the winery or the kitchen, in the fields or dairy, wherever they wanted him to be. He could imagine himself singing Compline. Once the idea settled in halfway through the retreat, he was thrilled. What meaning did his life have, anyway? A man lives with his mother and sleeps in his boyhood bed. He spends his day with small animals. In the evenings he reads of exotic places—Borneo, Antarctica, Egypt. He felt as if he had been living in a prologue, waiting for the text to begin. He went eagerly to his adviser, who asked him what he felt God wanted him to do.

"To pray," Riley answered. "To give my clumsy life over to—to those who would direct it."

"To what purpose?"

"Why, for my soul, and for God's pleasure," Riley answered. The words came easily. He was inspired.

"Sometimes what God wants most is devotion in one's ordinary life," the priest said.

Riley felt his heart sink. "I would love him only," he said. He had never touched a woman in any secret place. Not even the skirted thigh.

The priest wanted him to continue to pray as before and to read religious books, but most of all he admonished him to think of his daily life as an abandonment to God's will, and then—for surely the priest saw his stricken look, the look of a spurned suitor—in a year, if he felt the same, he was to return for another retreat. They would speak of it again then. If he had a calling, the priest said, God would keep the lines open.

That night he dreamed he was in an open field and the sky was rent with lightning. He dreamed he was afire but not consumed, dancing in the field and crying out like a madman.

When he returned home, the owner of the pet store where he had worked since high school told him he was ready to retire. He wanted to sell the store to Riley, whom he regarded as a son. The generous terms were feasible; it was another kind of call.

He went to Mass. He felt his Arkansas ardor waver. He had to decide about the store. He was his mother's support. What was so special about him or his life that he should withdraw from it?

He wrote to his adviser at the monastery, and the priest wrote back to say that good men were needed in the heartland.

A door swung shut. There was the store, the animals, his congregation. It was all less disappointing than he expected.

A
Christening

THE WRITING INSTRUCTOR TOLD RILEY to think of his memories as a storehouse of treasures. She spoke of memory as a gift. She said the sudden link between events, never thought of before, could bring a new sense of order to the past. She said half a writer's talent was receptivity. You just had to be open.

That night, lying on his bed, he shuffles through his memories like a deck of cards. The first time he struck a ball in the street with a board. That sense of power and possibility. That desire to repeat the act over and over again.

The night his mother pushed him toward his father's sickbed. "Kiss him good night," she said. "You may not have another chance." His father smelled like spearmint and sour milk. He was asleep. His skin was translucent; his cheekbones looked about to burst through. Riley was afraid. "Kiss him, kiss him!" his mother insisted. In the morning his father was dead.

He knows what he is doing.

He is avoiding the sharp clarity of his memory of Eva, though her memory is what he cherishes most. Avoiding the image of her moving across the bedroom toward the bathroom to get an antacid, turning with a puzzled expression, opening her mouth, then dropping where she stood, like a felled deer.

Postponing, he amends. Until he is ready to embrace her death as part of the experience of her. Until he is ready to let her go. His chest aches. Can he do both—let her go, and remember her? Can he do either?

He didn't stop to think what he might be asked to write in the class. He assumed the class was recreation. He thought perhaps they would describe the town in some way, or make up a little story about a villager they saw in the street. He thought they might build a more colorful vocabulary.

He watched the instructor speak to each student quietly. He waited his turn. When she came to him, she said, "Let the thoughts come freely. What is a betrayal? A broken trust."

He thought of his friend Patrick, in grade school. They were hardly ever apart. Then one day he was gone, off to seminary without a word. He never even asked if Riley were interested.

"I suppose I've been misunderstood," he said. He knew he had been. "But those who matter have been loyal." He was feeling guilty, the thought of Patrick. As if going off to serve God were a friend's abandonment.

Charlotte said, "Maybe what can't be helped seems a betrayal, think of that," and he knew he'd wanted to blame someone when Eva died. He looked at Charlotte and sighed. "Maybe next time," he said. He'd come to class hoping for something lighter. He wouldn't have minded a joke or two.

She said, "Maybe when you aren't thinking about it so hard," and smiled, and went on to another writer.

She was a little younger than he, a pretty woman with long dark hair worn in a braid like an Indian. Her simple blue cotton skirt and blouse made him think of nuns out of habit. She was thin, but she looked strong. She looked like a woman who had once done something difficult, who knew she could survive.

She said, "I want you to think about something for next week."

They all looked at her like birds waiting for a worm.

"Try to imagine a scene."

"A scene, Charlotte?" a woman said. "Like in a movie?"

Charlotte sat against a tabletop. "Something happens. The reader is there. Try to see your life caught in some moment. Think of it as a photograph suddenly in motion. Start with that lurch. Where does it take you? You are remembering, but you are also creating. There are no real facts, only the truth. Follow the moment."

The murmur in the room was the sound of soldiers sent on a minor mission. He felt the others' excitement. He was afraid of something, he didn't know what. He didn't know what he was doing, that was all. That was what a class was for, to learn something new. He resolved to try, if there was time, if he came back.

He met Eva at the christening of his neighbor Oscar Muñoz's twin granddaughters, children of a daughter. The party clustered on the church steps for photographs. Felipa Muñoz introduced them. They all trooped down the walk and across the street onto a shady sidewalk. The restaurant was three blocks away. Drivers of cars going by honked at them. They made a merry parade, the young parents leading the way with the babies' long white dresses trailing to their knees. The grandmothers carried armloads of flowers.

"I took Mrs. Iruegas and her mother to Fatima last year," Eva said.

"You are a godparent too?"

"And a travel agent," she said. "Avalon Tours, over on Belden. Here, take my card."

The restaurant had arranged long tables in a U shape and hung awnings to shade them from the midday sun. On the tables were photographs in silver frames—pictures of the couple on their wedding day, and studio portraits of the babies in their christening dresses. At each plate was a wallet-sized picture of the babies. Riley tucked his into a pocket. They had champagne in fluted glasses, and toasted the children and their parents.

Riley had consulted his Spanish teacher. He said, "To the great joy of tender babies," and everyone clapped.

Eva Wasierski said, "To family, community, and love," and they murmured approval. She had seated herself next to Mrs. Iruegas, with one of the young relatives on the other side.

Riley sat at the other table across the U from her. The waiters brought out a lavish lunch on white platters. Oscar's son wanted Riley's advice about dogs; his boys were begging for a puppy. Riley suggested they look at the pound first. Before he knew what had happened, he had agreed to go along. He realized suddenly that as godfather to these children, he would be part of the extended family, asked for advice and favors and companionship through the years. It pleased him to think it.

Mrs. Iruegas's old mother—everyone, relative or not, called her Abuela—put her cool dry hand on Riley's and leaned close to speak in a gravelly whisper. "The twins come from my side of the family." She spoke in Spanish, but with such precise enunciation, Riley understood quite well. She said, "My sister and I were identical. She died in a great flu epidemic along with Mama. Then my first baby was kicked in the head by a horse. The rider did not even stop to see what he had done."

"Life is hard," Riley said.

The old woman shook her finger in the direction of the babies. Their mother had removed the gowns and they lay in car seats on the tabletop, dressed in pink shirts and diapers, their feet wiggling in the warm air. "We never mix them up," Abuela said.

At first Riley did not understand. "The babies?" he asked.

The old woman cackled. She pointed to the pink-shirted twins. "Girl babies," she said. Then she wagged her finger toward Oscar, who had one of his twin grandsons on his lap, the child of his son. "Boy babies."

The band came in and began to play. People from inside the restaurant stood in the wide doorway or stepped off onto the court paving to watch. The babies' mother took one of the infants against her, and her mother helped her drape a fine cotton shawl elaborately over her shoulder and the child so that her breast was not exposed by nursing. Half a dozen little children ran around wildly, inspired, no doubt, by the riotous tunes from the musicians, who wore starched shirts and broad scarlet cummerbunds. The babies' father took his own mother to the center of the courtyard, where the paving stones were smoothest. She was laughing and shaking her head. Oscar went over to the musicians and spoke to them. They began playing a sweet melodic song. Oscar helped his wife up from her chair to dance.

Riley made his way to Eva Wasierski. There was something almost formidable about her—her wide eyes, her carefully arranged brown hair. She had the look of someone used to authority, like a school principal.

The chair next to her was empty now, and at the last

moment his courage left him and he sat down instead of asking her to dance. He said, "It's a nice party, isn't it?"

She smiled and nodded. She was watching the dancing couples. One fat uncle was mopping his forehead with a large handkerchief.

"Have you known them long?" Riley asked.

"They are all frequent flyers," she said. "I have sent these ladies to Guadalajara many times."

"I've never been."

"To Mexico?"

"Anywhere," he blurted, then regretted it. She would know him for the boring man he was.

"You've missed the summer sales." She was giving him her full attention now. "But fall is the best time to travel anyway."

"I don't have any plans—"

"Planning is my vocation. Now, do you dance, Mr. Riley?"

An
Independent Stroll

IN THE DEPTH OF HIS MUSING, he falls into a dreamless sleep, then wakes at dawn.

Most of the posada guests are early risers. By the time he returns from a brisk walk, many of the dining tables are occupied, and the cheerful sounds of voices and the clink of silverware and china ring through the room.

"Over here, young fellow!"

Riley recognizes a man he met the day before in the writing workshop. The man takes Riley by the elbow and steers him to his wife. Les and Kitty. They fill him in on their year-long routine. Winter here, spring with their son's family in Albuquerque, summer at an old lakeside house in Idaho. "It's a good life," Les says. Riley nods, as he feels he must. He wonders what happened to fall.

He orders one of the local rolls smeared with beans and cheese.

"They'll do an American breakfast," Kitty says. "On Tuesday nights, they do pot roast and pie."

"Sometimes I miss the stones," Les says dreamily. When Riley looks up puzzled, he says, "I owned jewelry stores."

Riley chews his tasty roll while he hears about fifty years in jewelry. Kitty is wearing several extravagant rings.

"We're putting together a group to go see the monarch butterflies," Les says. "We'll put you down. There's a Canadian lives here, knows it all. He'll go with us."

"I don't know how long I'll be here," Riley says.

"You only just got here!" Kitty says. He sees she has added his name to her list in a tiny spiral notebook lying by her saucer. Meekly, he says, "I'm in pets. Puppies, kittens, gerbils. Turtles, finches, parakeets. Nothing exotic."

"Exotic," Les whispers. "Look at that."

He points up. Riley turns to see one of the maids crossing the balcony carrying a string mop. She wears a short pink uniform, and her hair is wrapped in a white cloth. Her short skirt reveals long, lithe legs. She moves with an easy swing of the hips, like someone walking along a path.

"Now, Les," Kitty scolds affectionately. She looks at Riley and shakes her head. "These silly men, they check out all the girls."

Riley's face must show his dismay, because she quickly adds, "I think they do it mostly to goad us wives. It doesn't mean a thing."

Les says, "Oh, hell, no, it's all hands off. I think the management would kick you out if you said boo to one of their maids. But that one—she's a beauty. You'd think she could turn it to some better use."

Riley drinks the last cold drop of his coffee and excuses himself. He climbs the long staircase to the second floor, feeling observed. He doesn't mean to be critical. It's just too early for chitchat. Les and Kitty are fine people. Friendly.

He crosses the balcony. Near his room he stops and looks down on the lobby. Some of the breakfast tables are just below him; he sees a table with four people. One says something, and they are all laughing.

He should have planned things more. Maybe a little tour. Instead, he's come with no more destination than the name of the hotel. His vacation is up to him to fill. Yesterday he felt buoyant with anticipation. Already he bobs in his aimlessness.

When he first introduced Eva to Margaret, his sister said, "She knows just what to do with you," with obvious suspicion. It was because Eva was Polish. Margaret got over it, though she was right.

He lets himself into his room almost stealthily, as if someone were asleep in there. He lies on his side across the bed, his knees tucked up slightly. He has not drawn open the shades, and the room is still dark and cool. He pulls a pillow to his chest.

When he is feeling better, he goes out again and walks beyond the town center, across the main highway, up onto the hillside where there are clusters of humble homes, mostly limewashed brick or stucco. A few houses are painted bright blue or yellow. He walks between the houses through wide alleys where chickens scrabble in the dust. A goat is tethered on a long rope to a scrawny tree behind a wooden fence. A little boy nearby is rolling a hoop. Another comes along behind him kicking a can. Two baby boys in short shirts, their bottoms bare, stand in a doorway. They peek at him from behind their tiny hands. He waves.

Beside a tree a girl of seven or eight stands watching him. She wears a T-shirt that says PUERTO RICO, and blue shorts. She is balanced on one leg; the other crosses it at the knee so that her bare foot sticks out to the side. She is openly curious, with a steady gaze. Riley pauses in the center of the path twenty feet away. She tilts her head the slightest bit. Behind her a woman appears in the roofed lean-to next to a tiny, square, flat-roofed house. She wears a print cotton dress like his mother used to wear, and a ruffled apron tied at the waist. Riley sees now that there is a spiral of smoke coming from under the roof. Behind the woman is some kind of stove, probably with coals, and across a rack, a flat iron pan.

Riley would like to speak to the girl and the woman. He would like to ask why the child is not in school and what the woman is preparing in her alfresco kitchen. But he realizes suddenly that he is an intruder in a neighborhood, that he has no right to wander these paths. He picks up his pace. As he walks by the woman, he nods. She stands with her fists on her hips. Like the girl, she has no expression at all.

He clambers down the side of a hill, sliding the last few yards, barely keeping on his feet. Between him and the highway now is only a dry gully. He climbs through it. As he reaches the side of the road, he hears a long alarming honk. An open Jeep roars to a stop near him.

"Riley!" It is the writer, Charlotte Amory.

"Hop in," she says. She tells him she has been to the city to buy art supplies. "I thought that was you sliding down that hill," she says. "Off exploring?"

"Gawking."

He turns toward the center of the town. Several streets are hung with flapping plastic banners. "What's all that?" he asks.

"A fiesta, a few weeks ago. Every year they clean the statue of the Virgin in the church, then celebrate it. Eventually someone will take the stuff down. Probably when they want to put something else up."

"I'm sorry I missed it."

"You can always find a fiesta. Tecatitlán has one coming up soon. Say, are you hungry? I'm starved. Let's go to the Patio again. You've got to try Consolata's *tortas*."

The Patio is along a side street off the square close to the market. It is a single three-walled room in a concrete building, open to the sidewalk, with metal shutters to pull down when it is closed. There is a grill and a bar with stools around two sides of it, a couple of tiny tables, and a few more on the sidewalk. In the corner are two coolers, and between them, tucked in as if part of the furnishings, a very old woman garbed in a black dress and shawl sits snoozing on a low chair.

Riley and Charlotte peer over the bar to see what's cooking. Spicy sausages, split frankfurters, thin tough-looking slabs of beef, odd meats Riley doesn't recognize, and onions sputtering and steaming on the grill. Riley takes a *torta* with avocado and cheese.

"Goodness, you could eat that at home in an art museum," Charlotte says. "Didn't you come here for a little spice?" She points to a meat she says is pork, and requests hot peppers on the side.

Riley gives his belly a pat. "My system tells me, proceed with caution."

They take their beers and sit at a table on the sidewalk. They have a good view of the strollers on the square. Vendors have set up around the bandstand, selling candles, pork rinds, trinkets, holy cards, comic books, and many other items. Here and there a man goes by carrying boxes as big as he is, or cages of birds or chickens.

Riley laughs aloud. "Will you look at that?" he says, and Charlotte does.

She laughs and says, "I bet they're not for any Mexicans."

Riley has spied a young man in wide white flapping pants, carrying a stacked column of shiny white bedpans down the street.

The cook brings their lunch. Charlotte dangles a jalapeño. "Come on, one little bite," she coaxes, but Riley laughs and says maybe another time. She eats the pepper, and tears spurt onto her cheeks.

"The secret," she says in a strangled voice, "is to take bread, not beer, after." Which she does.

"Oh, all right, one little bite," Riley says. Charlotte cuts off the tip of her second pepper. Riley pops it onto his tongue. His eyes smart, his mouth burns, but it's not so bad. Not impossible. He doesn't really taste it. "You don't run into these at the hotel," he says. "You have to ask for them specially."

"I lived at the Posada Celestial for a while, when I first came to Lago de Luz," Charlotte says. "Then I moved into the Great House where I live now, in the village. I've been there four years."

"The Great House?"

"It was once the house of a hacienda. Now it belongs to a factory owner from Guadalajara. He has restored one wing beautifully. Another wing was converted into a residential school for deaf children. It's a wonderful place. You will come see it."

"In Tecatitlán?"

Charlotte nods.

"I was there before. There was a priest there. A Spaniard, with blue eyes."

"Father Luis. Luis Bernal. He's still there."

"I'm surprised. He seemed a man of considerable education. I thought he would go to a city, maybe back to Europe. We did some chores for him, my wife Eva and I. Some paperwork. He was so grateful for such a small thing."

"We're friends," Charlotte says. "In a tiny Indian village, there are not so many people who read. I lend him books. He prays for my soul. It is a good trade."

"Maybe I'll go see him." Riley's sudden sadness shows.

Charlotte pats his hand. "You are going to tell me why you've come to Lago, aren't you, Thomas Riley? I'm a good listener. I never make judgments or give advice. And I like an interesting story."

"That would hardly be mine."

"I think it would. Besides, you are alone here. You need a friend. You must come to Tecatitlán. I will have you and Father Luis to the Great House for supper. He will come, then."

Riley chews thoughtfully. In a few moments he goes to fetch two more beers. When he is seated again, he says slowly, "It was just this time of the year. We went to the market, but there was nothing to buy. There was a bridge tournament, but we didn't care to play. We went to the little village to look around. We walked every street."

Good
Intentions

THE RILEYS MET FATHER BERNAL outside the village church and invited him to lunch. He was blue-eyed and skinny; he looked as if he could use a good meal. He said he had recently arrived in Mexico, had only been in the village a few months. He spoke English carefully and well, with a faint lilt. He excused himself to change into cotton trousers and a gray-blue polo shirt. Over a lunch of goat stew, he told them he had discovered a drawerful of letters stuffed in there by the old priest who had preceded him.

"He didn't speak English. He barely read or wrote Spanish. And here was all this correspondence. Checks. Seminarians offering seasons of ministry. A church in California wanting to be a sister congregation. Children who had grown up here and gone away sent donations. Who knows how people hear of a humble village? They are far away. They imagine themselves bringing things to poor people. It's all good intentions."

Mrs. Riley said, "Perhaps we could help."

They went through the letters and made two piles in two languages. They said they would answer all of those that were in English.

Mrs. Riley bought cards in a shop in Lago de Luz, and they came back the next day. In her lovely Palmer handwriting, she wrote on each:

> *If you should appear sometime, the village would receive you. If you have skills and a large heart, the people will welcome you. If you have money, spend it where you see the need.*

She passed the card to Mr. Riley, and he wrote, above the place where the priest would sign: "In Christ's name, for the parish of the brown-skinned Virgin."

Across the last card, Mr. Riley leaned to kiss his wife. She was so many things he admired: kind, discreet, curious. Brave, in her way. He had forgotten what it was like to be alone. He did not then imagine a world without her.

Eusebio

THOUGH THEY COULD WALK ALL THE WAY FROM THE VILLAGE to the mesa by the road, they like to cross through the brush and climb to an outcrop they think of as their own. Eusebio always comes behind so that he might break the fall if either of the girls should slip on the small rocks and steep incline. Divina goes first, eager and agile as a goat, her long black hair flying out over the billows of her white blouse and long red skirt. She carries her boombox, a gift from the American woman Charlotte Amory. Between them, Eusebio's tiny sister Yzelda carries three oranges in a string bag.

It is early evening. They settle on the rock and look out over the village. Tendrils of smoke rise from the charcoal fires where beans are simmering and skillets smoking, waiting for tortillas to warm. The spire of the church of the Virgin peeks above dense clusters of tree branches. Beyond the village are the mountains. They cannot see the square from their perch, but houses and huts hug the hillside in good view. A fresh breeze cools their hot faces. Below them the women do women things. The men, in from the fields, change to clean shirts and then saunter along the plaza for their pulque or beer before supper. No one will miss the young folk for a while.

Divina puts a tape into her silver machine. Yzelda arranges herself like a child, her head in Divina's lap. Eusebio aches with jealousy and longing, but he sits as he climbed, one girl removed from the one he loves.

"It is time for you to choose a wife," his mother said on Sunday. She insisted he go to the square. A mariachi band was playing and everyone was out. Girls strolled arm in arm, giggling and preening, while boys walked the other way with a swagger. Eusebio is too old for this. He does not wish to play at love. He turned nineteen just last month, half a year older than Divina. His mother was right, it is time, but he wants only the honey of Divina's lips. And there is something more. He wants to leave Tecatitlán.

A week ago he stood on the highway and waited with Divina for the bus to take her into Guadalajara. A girl from the village, Aleida, was working there as maid to a family in a fine apartment building. Divina was going to see what she might do. "Come, come," Aleida begged her the last time she was home. She was lonely for home, but she would never return for good. She told Divina, "You speak English, you could work for an American family and make good money. You can sleep with me on my cot while you look." She touched her friend's hair. "The Americans, they like a pretty girl in the house."

Eusebio thought if Divina took such employment he would find work in the city, too. He is good with his hands. He would learn to work with machines. In a year or two they could have an apartment of their own. They could marry. He had not yet had the courage to say all this, but hadn't they spoken for years of going away? Weren't some things understood? They had grown up almost like brother and sister, friends and neighbors since childhood and school. They had slipped imperceptibly into new affection. People saw them together and thought nothing of it; they had kissed in the orchard and laughed about it. Hadn't she scorned all the boys who admired her beauty? She knew nothing would change here. All the smart young people went away. And those other boys—who knew what they were thinking?

His mother said no one would marry Divina because her mother, Consolata, was a witch. "How can you say that?" he demanded. His mother said it was because Consolata had had three husbands. The village said they had all died, but no one knew that for sure. "And that doesn't count Don Genaro the grocer," his mother added. "Who is, of course, alive." Then Eusebio's father told her to put a prune in her mouth and stop her foolish gossip in front of the boy.

Wasn't that interesting? In that moment, he was a boy, in front of his parents, but he was man enough to need a wife, man enough to work his father's field, to care for animals and carry wood and water.

Yzelda hums a little of the tune from Divina's tape. She reaches into her bag for the oranges. Divina takes two, and as she peels one, dropping the rind into her lap, she passes plump bites across Yzelda to Eusebio.

The fruit is sweet, but as he swallows what Divina gives him, tears spring to his eyes.

"What does he sing?" Yzelda asks. She sucks at her orange greedily.

"His name is Sting," Divina says. "He loves a woman impossibly." She hands the rest of an orange to Eusebio. The second orange rolls down her skirt. She catches it with a turn of her foot.

"Steeng," says Yzelda.

"The singer," Divina says. "Not the man."

She lies back on the rock, baring her long throat. Eusebio scrapes a piece of orange rind with his teeth.

"Ro—xanne," Yzelda sings. She sounds foolish. She sniffles. She is bound to be thinking of Reymundo, her boyfriend who left on the back of a water truck months and months ago and never came back.

Eusebio thinks, *I should have gone with him.*

Maybe Reymundo crossed the northern border. Perhaps he is in California right now. He eats meat every day and drinks clean water. He thinks of Tecatitlán as a tale he is forgetting.

Yzelda says, "This must be the most beautiful place in the world."

Divina retrieves the orange, then props herself up on her elbows and looks out at the sunset.

"Aiee, what's so beautiful?" scoffs Eusebio, though he could easily have agreed. It is for this, and companionship, that they have come. No one is poor up here. The village is a jewel.

"Why, the mountains, that are blue by day and purple at dusk, then black in the night," Yzelda says.

"There are mountains all over Mexico!" Eusebio says. "There are mountains all over the world."

Yzelda spits seeds and turns her head away from her testy brother. She looks like a pouting doll.

Divina says, "My brother says there are rolling hills where he lives in Texas. There are many flowers and trees."

"There are flowers here," Eusebio grumbles. "For all the good it does when your plot is bare." In fact, his father's land has a small orchard and decent soil, but it is not enough for a second son's family, and his brother has two babies and another on the way.

"Did your brother write?" Yzelda asks eagerly.

Divina says, "Yes, a card at Christmas. Mama put it on her altar. She prays he will come for fiesta."

"Maybe Reymundo will come for fiesta," Yzelda says.

Eusebio pounds his fist on his thigh. "Who cares!"

Yzelda says, "My papa says he will grow a mustache and wear out the soles of his shoes, then he will come home to work the land."

"Corn and beans and squash! Is that a life?" Eusebio says.

Yzelda answers quietly. "Children grow on it. Since the Revolution it is our own and not part of a hacienda."

"The Revolution! One day soon I will go to the city. And Divina—what about you?"

"The city is not far enough," Divina replies. "I do not wish to sleep on the roof of a building. I want to sleep on a bed in a white house."

"Who has such a house?" the other girl asks.

"I will ask my brother to take me to Texas. I wish to work in the white house of gringos. I will wash clothes and dishes in machines and bathe with water that comes hot from the faucet."

"You will be lonely," Yzelda scolds.

"You will still be a maid," Eusebio says bitterly.

Divina plops the orange back into Yzelda's bag. She turns off the tape recorder and stands. "It is time to go down," she says.

"Time to go," Eusebio says. "Oh yes, it is time."

The anger he feels just now scalds away his longing for Divina, though the anger will fade and the longing will return. She cannot see what anyone can see: that her brother will never come back, that he would not take her if he did. That her beauty in a strange land would be misunderstood and misused. That what they might do together she cannot do alone.

He starts off toward the road. "Hurry, before it is dark," he calls over his shoulder. "Careful how you step."

"Ro—xanne," Yzelda sings over and over. Divina knows the words. She goes on with the song.

A
Slight Incline

IN THE MORNING, Divina ties the rope of her hair at her neck and dresses in her pink uniform. On the cooking patio she sits with her mother to drink coffee with condensed milk and to eat a few tortillas. She tells her mother, "Tía Filomena did not wake this morning. All night she snored like a horse and wore herself out."

For as long as she can remember she has felt the warm breath of the old woman on her back at night, and she does not mind the sound of it.

Her mother says, "Put a plate on the table by the bed. Put coffee in a jug on the floor. It is time for us to go."

In Lago de Luz, Tom Riley rises and dresses in soft old sweatpants and shirt, then opens the shutters. He gazes for a moment toward the nightstand and the photograph of his wife at the dry fountain. Sadness sits in him like a lump, but it doesn't fill his body. In the morning, he wakes glad to be alive.

*   *   *

Is it fortune or design that sends him out on his morning walk just as Consolata and Divina Arispe struggle up the slight incline of the promenade toward the market and the cafe?

Some might say, It is God's hand.

Riley sets out, a man who makes the best of every day, expecting little but the pleasure of his body in motion, and the sharp fruity smells of the street as he approaches the market, the prospect of a trip later in the week to some interesting site.

Already he has called his sister Margaret to say that Lago de Luz has not changed. It is still beautiful. And all around the lake, he told her, there are things to see. Fiestas and artisans' workshops. Ex-haciendas and churches. Oh yes, he teased her, there are many places here to pray!

She said, I hope that makes you happy, Tom.

He does not expect to be happy, only absorbed.

He sees the woman from the *torta* shop ahead of him, and though he has only seen her twice, he recognizes her by the washed indigo of her skirt and the peculiar knotting of her apron. She turns toward an alley. Her face, in profile, confirms her identity. She walks with a quiet, easy stride. She carries her chin high; her hair, in the sunshine, gleams.

He sees, too, the younger woman, familiar but not recognized, a pretty girl with her arms full of string bags of onions and tomatoes.

He thinks to himself, as they turn the corner, that he will have lunch at the *torta* shop. He has a destination for the middle of the day. He springs ahead, feeling better than a moment ago, seizing whatever presents itself, because he is a traveler and he has come for this.

He thinks, I will ask the señora for a recommendation. "Not too hot," I'll say, "but not a gringo's sandwich, you know?" He is thinking of the meats cut in unfamiliar ways.

Such a small thing, not even an encounter. Two peasant women and a gringo on the avenue. A little bit of luck.

In the lobby, a long table has been set up in preparation for the tour buses. At one end, a woman tidies a pile of flyers: SHOULD YOU LIVE IN LAGO? FACTS ABOUT REAL ESTATE. At the other end, a man Riley recognizes from the Lakeside Society Library is selling a guidebook to the region. *A Traveler's Treasury*, it is called. Riley looks one over, then buys it.

"Canadian fellow wrote it," the man tells him. "He knows his stuff. He's lived here nearly twenty years."

"Great," Riley says. Just flipping the pages, he can tell the book is full of information about places he'd never have heard about. "I'd like to see some villages." He thinks of them as mysterious places, with secrets he will never know.

"Come by the library, too. Usually somebody's been where you want to go. Ask for me. Henry—"

"Tom Riley." They shake hands.

"I thought so!" A voice booms behind him. "Tom Riley. It is you, isn't it? You haven't got a gray hair, you sonofagun."

He turns and sees a man he knew at the hotel before, with Eva. Joe Flaxman. The two couples had hit it off at breakfast one day. They went in the Flaxmans' car to a fiesta in the mountains. They stood near the plaza; below them they could see smoky bonfires lighting the parade route. Later they danced, switching partners back and forth, drinking spiked pomegranate punch. Days later, Eva told Riley that Joe had kissed her. For luck. Riley's face had shown his shock; it made Eva laugh.

He remembers exactly what she said: "A big wet smooch, here, on the corner of the mouth." He had wanted to wipe it away.

Flaxman is standing in front of a large framed display of

photographs of the town from the turn of the century. All the subjects are city people, the women in long dresses with high bosoms.

"The wife and I are here for the winter," Flaxman says. "Came in last night." He twists his gold band around and around his finger. "But—a new wife," he says. "We were married last August. Alice died."

"I'm so sorry to hear that." Riley looks at Flaxman's shoes. They are a new pale color. Used to be, there were no shoes that color. Blue, but not really. And that leather that's not shiny. "I know how hard—you see, Eva, too. I lost her, a year and a half ago."

Flaxman is surprised. He is older, a man already retired when they met, when the Rileys, newlyweds, were young. He shakes his head. "You don't say," he says. "Not Eva."

Riley's attention drifts to a photograph of two slender women with parasols, stepping into a rowboat. "It was sudden." He wants to say something more. Dead wives—is there so little to say? They could talk about being alone. It's not what you expect; you always hear the women will outlive you. But Joe Flaxman is not alone. And what would Riley say to a man who once kissed his wife?

A little later, Riley comes downstairs to sit by the pool with his book. He is reading *The Plumed Serpent,* by D. H. Lawrence. He is finding it fascinating and slightly offensive, as if he is a stand-in for the Indians who never even knew the book existed. Lawrence, he thinks, must have been a very sensual and romantic and arrogant man.

He has changed into khaki pants and a T-shirt. At a table, two men are playing cards. Flaxman, stretched out in a deck chair, waves him over, reaching with his other hand to stay the movement of a woman stepping to the edge of the pool. The wife.

Her name is Brenda. She has a pleasant, friendly face.

Her hair is cut short with a soft fringe on her forehead. She is much younger than her husband, younger, probably, than Riley. She shakes his hand. "At home, I do ten laps four times a week," she says, and laughs heartily. "Here I ought to be able to pull it off every day, huh?" The pool is only long enough for five or six strokes.

Flaxman beams. "Sit, sit, take a load off," he tells Riley. He tells him he has heard there is a first-class boxing match coming up in Guadalajara. Maybe Riley would want to go?

"I just can't," Brenda says. "Smashing each other in the face—ugh. I'll fish. I'll try that. But not boxing, not for me."

Riley shrugs. "It's not my sport, either."

Flaxman is not so easily deterred. He says he remembers when Cassius Clay took the world championship. "I was on the coast, north of Acapulco. No resorts up there then. We listened on shortwave radio, an old navy captain and I. Even Alice got excited. It was contagious. You knew he was making history."

Both of the men shift in their chairs. Brenda sits on the edge of the pool, dangling her legs in the water. A plastic slat, loose from its weave, slaps the paving beneath Riley's seat. "It's a tough thing, to box," he says. "To put your body out there, so scarcely protected. Do you think they ever like it? Is it ever fun?"

"They like it when they win!" Flaxman says. "They like it when they're young and tough. I watched a match last year in San Blas. Two dwarfs, you believe that? And women wrestlers, same bill. It was all choreographed, like a dance. Not very good, but something to see, nevertheless. I always try to go where there's sport. Hell, I'll watch kids play soccer. I like the competition." His wife slides into the water and kicks off in a backstroke. He settles himself lower in his chair. "Muhammad Ali, he is now. I saw him in an airport last year. Beautiful guy. Sick, you know? Too bad." His wife bobs up at the other end and waves. He gives her a salute.

In a few moments he is dozing. Riley moves over to the mineral pool. Several women are sitting on the steps, immersed to their shoulders. They hold their heads high, careful with their hair.

He sits by a table and opens his book. He has been thinking about renting a car, but it would be pleasant to visit some towns by bus. Not to worry about driving, gas, the roads. There are sights to see. Eva said the world is a place you look at while you are looking for yourself.

He looks over and sees Flaxman, awake, and he waves, and nods. *Yes. Yes, I will go. Yes, they are dead.*

She is dead.

Eva's lips were cool and dry. Sometimes he probed gently with the tip of his tongue. He doesn't think she ever liked that much. Always, her breath was sweet.

The guidebook has an insert, a foldout map of the lake region. Riley sits on a stool at the Patio counter and traces the highways with his finger as he reads descriptions in the book. *The arches support an ancient aqueduct. A few steps away is the hacienda chapel, in good condition . . . Near here, the scenery changes, giving way to fertile fields of beans and cabbages . . .* He eats a sausage *torta* and asks for a second beer. They come in small bottles, not quite as cold as he likes. Sometimes he looks up and watches the señora at her work. She works quickly, but her gestures are so graceful and efficient, her work is a kind of ballet. A few times, she glances his way. She smiles slightly, not really looking at him. Maybe her smile is contentment, he thinks. He hopes that is so. Didn't Charlotte say the woman owned the cafe?

We have things in common, he thinks. Entrepreneurial experiences. In his head he hears himself say, *How's busi-*

ness been? He has hardly thought of the pet store in days. Of course, it is in good hands. His assistant, Dora Benson, has been with him for nearly fifteen years, since she was in high school.

He drinks another cold beer as the señora cleans up. He watches her wiping out her pots and dishes. He used to sit at the kitchen table as Eva worked. He offered to help—they didn't have a dishwasher, and he could dry—but she said no, she liked to do it herself. She liked him there behind her, maybe talking, maybe not. Every few months he helped her with the floor, both of them on their hands and knees with soft brushes. They had laid a floor of dark green tiles, and painted the walls clean white. Cleared of his mother's old furniture, the house had a fresh, airy feel. Eva took all the heavy curtains down and replaced them with pleated linen blinds that rolled silently.

The house without her was so empty, he had invited his nephew Derek to live with him while he was attending college. There was Derek's music in the house now. There were his friends, coming and going, young people with odd hair and bright clothes and a cloud of laughter and intrigue about them.

"Is there something more I can serve you?" the señora asks. She has a curious, kind expression. He realizes that the lunch business is over; everyone else has come and gone. Her bowls and baskets are stacked neatly. He stands up and brushes the front of his shirt, then closes his guidebook. He smooths the map.

"It's beautiful country around here," he says.

Her smile now is warm and surprised. "How well you speak Spanish, Señor."

He blushes. "If we speak slowly."

"Where will you go?" She points at the map.

He turns it so that they can both see. "There are so

many places. I am thinking here, to the south of the lake."

She moves a little closer. "Is there a village on the map—"
She peers at it, names a place, an old, Indian name. He doesn't
see it, though.

"Do you know what town it is near?"

"Oh yes, of course," she says. She names one. "And the
village, it is also called Saint Mary of Tears."

"I did see that on the map." He taps the place. "Here is
the village. Here is the town. The book says there is a small
museum there, with rock carvings, and an old sail-canoe. Do
you know the town?"

"I was in the church a few times as a girl. I saw the earthquake paintings. Sometimes we went in for market. I was
born in the village, I grew up there. I have been here a long
time now."

"You have visited the village since you left?"

"Never."

"Well." He is so awkward. He folds the map.

"In the chapel, Señor—"

"Yes?"

"There is a weeping Virgin."

"A statue?"

"Yes, the Virgin. Sometimes she grants your heart's wish."

"And sometimes not?"

"She sees a wider picture," she says sadly.

"So my wife used to tell me."

"You will come again?"

"Often," he replies. "There are so many foods for me to
try." So many things he has not done.

Dreamer

DIVINA CHANGED IN MY ROOM, then came out onto the back veranda, which I was using as a studio. I had hung bamboo shades on two sides. The light came from the long back exposure, where the porch looked out onto the orchard, thick with orange, papaya, and mango trees, and coffee bushes. At that time of the day, the sun dappled through the branches of the trees, but there was one open wash of light onto the porch, and there I had placed the chair for Divina.

A year ago, on a visit to San Miguel de Allende, I had bought a cotton kimono for her. It was deep blue, with green and purple peacocks. She sat at the table, her legs drawn up under the kimono, and reached around, her chin resting on her knee, and cut off bites of mango daintily, with a fork. Her long hair was down, free from its knot, but caught loosely with a red velvet cord I had hung on the hook with the garment.

Under the table, the house's old white dog, Loza, lay in a lazy lump, and Divina nestled the toes of her feet against his back. Now and then the dog heaved a sigh, shuddered, and settled again into satisfied repose.

I was puttering by the easel. There was always this time between us at the beginning of our afternoon session, a quarter hour or so when she might have been the lady of the house, moving calmly through an afternoon ritual of refreshment. She understood that I was nervous, that I had to ease my way like someone dipping into cold water. In the first weeks when I had begun to draw her, she had been curious, had wanted to see what I was doing, and to inspect the products of our sessions. Before long, she stopped inquiring; in the three years she had been my model, I never saw her try to steal a glance, or look at anything propped against the wall. Yet when once in a while I showed her something, she expressed delight. "Oh, look!" she'd say, "it's my hand exactly. It's my foot." Or she would peer closely: "Do I really look like that, so sour, like an old lawyer?" Of course she did not look like an old anything. The sweet plumpness of her adolescence had become womanliness. I thought she was very much aware of it. I thought she probably did not know what to do with it. She never spoke of suitors. We never talked about love. Maybe I was too old for that, too. Except for the occasional visits of my landlord, Elias Santos, I lived like a nun. In the village they called me the widow. I had never had an opportunity to correct them. Gossip is always just below the surface, and never rises before its subject.

I arranged the turpenoid, the brushes and jars, just so. I was painting in black and white. Grisaille. I had explained it to her—that later, I would add layers of paint called glazes. I would add the color. First, I would make the drawing perfect.

I had been working on the painting for a couple of months. I dreamed about it often—funny, because it was modeled on a photograph of a girl dreaming. And when I dreamed about it, I was never the girl, I was always outside—myself, I guess, asking her what she saw, where she went.

While Divina began telling me about her recent trip to Guadalajara, she wrapped her feet, like the girl in the photograph on which my painting was modeled. She wound strips of gauze, first around the ankle, then under the arch of each foot. Under her kimono, she wore a simple cotton shift that I had had the village seamstress make from my sketch. It was something like a man's sleeveless undershirt, lengthened, but of a much finer, gauzy material for which I had searched one whole day in the city.

When Divina saw the photograph by Manuel Bravo, she just laughed and said she would lie naked on a rug if I wanted, as long as the gardener could not see. I told her it wasn't necessary. The shift was beautiful on her, and very revealing, and I told myself that it was my painting, not Bravo's photograph, I was making. I could not tell if she was disappointed or relieved. It occurred to me that she must think of me as an aunt, someone her mother's age; she had no reason to be shy with me, after so much time. I had done hundreds of drawings of her, many of them with her body draped and much exposed, but I had never asked her to pose nude, though of course I had seen her, had arranged the cloths over her just so.

She was telling me about the life of her friend Aleida, who lived in a concrete room on the roof of a building.

"She has one free day a week. We went to the zoo together. She liked the monkeys. I liked the giraffes. I liked their long necks. She was wearing sandals, with set-in colored glass. She told me about the city, how you can go into a store and there are fifty lipsticks. Comic books. She comes home every five or six weeks. Doesn't she miss her mother? Why would she live like that, like a prisoner on the rooftop, for shoes and lipsticks?"

I motioned for her to lie on the chaise. It was made of wicker, and I had draped a dark purple-red cloth on it. She tossed the kimono onto the back of a chair, and stretched out. She crossed one leg over the other at the knee, like in the photograph. She pulled her arm up and tucked her hand under her neck.

"I don't want to live on a roof," she said. "I want to live in a room with a window. Gringos don't put their maids on top of the building like that, do they?"

"I've never known anyone with a live-in maid. Maybe in L.A. or New York. I'd think they live in the house or apartment. Listen, Divina, you wouldn't like it in New York, you know? It's cold. It's a very, very hard place to live."

She thought that was funny. "I don't want to go there. I just want to go to Texas, where my brother lives."

I almost asked the question she had just raised about her friend: Wouldn't you miss your mother? I knew she was the heart of Consolata's life. I thought of it a lot, the closeness of a mother and daughter. The mother, I thought, was the means of survival, but the child was the reason to live.

With her arm up in position, Divina's breast diminished into a smooth mound beneath the shift, the round curve of it showing along the edge. I remembered that I had set aside a few fashion magazines for her. She loved them. Sometimes she would strike a model's pose for me: Look, Charlotte, is this right? Look, Charlotte, she'd say, with her hip thrust forward, her mouth in a pout. She would have made a good photographer's model.

"Do I need to close my eyes?"

I shook my head. "I'm working on the raised leg." The light washed the outside curve of her bent leg. On the inside, where her calf pressed against her thigh, the flesh was deeply shadowed. The shift fell back off the thigh, then draped over the other hip and shone white in a shaft of sharp light. I wanted the painting to be a kind of consciousness of that area, the mystery inside the triangle of her bent leg that seemed to rise from her lower belly, the far hip out of sight, the pudendum and the mound shrouded in cloth. I worked very slowly. I felt my breath. And all the time she chatted softly, happily, as comfortable in her pose as a napping child.

I was thinking that next I would do a portrait of her. I wanted to paint her green eyes and her coppery cheeks.

"I saw a little dog today, in one of the rooms. It had a face the size of a cup, but with so much hair! All the time I was in the room, the dog ran from corner to corner of the bed and barked at me. When I tried to change the sheets, it snarled."

"What did you do?" She was sure to have changed the bed.

"I went down to the kitchen for a piece of meat, and I held it, like this—" She dangled her free hand over her face. "It jumped up and down, begging, and then I took the meat across the room, across the door of the bath, until it followed me. Then I threw it—so fast!—into the shower, and pulled the door shut. I made the bed and got out of there."

I laughed.

"Then, as I was putting everything into the closet downstairs, ready to go to my house, the manager came, oh so angry, and shouted at me. He yells at us every day for something. Like a big patron. The señora had come to him about me. About locking the dog up in the bathroom." She giggled, so I knew it had turned out all right. "I said I would tell her I was sorry."

She pushed up, nearly sitting. "When I found the señora, out in the garden, I saw the dog was under her chair. I told her I was sorry, if I scared her pet. 'It's not me you need to tell!' she said, and she picked her dog up and held it against her chest. Its bottom legs wiggled, like a swimming bug. I had to tell that terrible little dog I was sorry! Do you believe it?" She lay back down. At some point, she had stopped laughing. So had I.

A Night
in the Country

THE FIRST THING RILEY DID WHEN HE ARRIVED IN TAPALPA was to
look for a hotel and make a reservation for that night. He
could have made it back to Lago de Luz, but this town had a
lovely plaza, with a bandstand and high, graceful trees. In
the evening, the townspeople would be out. He would enjoy
seeing the families with their children dressed up, and young
sweethearts feigning indifference.

He ate lunch at the hotel across from the plaza, then
made his way to the museum. The rock carvings mentioned
in the guidebook were photographs; the originals, the plac-
ard said, were inaccessible mountain sites. *Well, yes,* he
thought. What was he expecting? It would be terrible to tear
up a cliff, a mountain, an outcrop of rock, even if you could.
Still, he would like to see some petroglyphs. He would check
the guidebook again, he would ask around at the Lakeside
Society, to find out where it was possible to view some. If he
couldn't make it this trip, he would go the next time.

He was standing before photographs of little stick con-
quistadors on horses. What a surprise they must have been
to the Indians. He'd heard somewhere—it must have been in
Santa Fe, when he and Eva went to an arts fair there—that
the natives of the Americas had thought that each Spaniard
and his horse was a single being, with six legs.

In Tapalpa, the guidebook said, there were pre-Hispanic
carvings. So much to see. The realization that he could come
back to the region—that the intention to return had already
been forming in him—that was a six-legged surprise, too.
Why not? Eva had taught him how easy it is to go from one
place to another. She said once, "Boston, Paris, Cairo. The
difference in travel is just a matter of hours on a plane. An
itinerary is just a wish list made practical. We can go anywhere we want. Eastern Europe, Russia. See how it has all
opened up."

He read in his book about the town and its church. There
had been an earthquake 150 years earlier. The chapel was
spared damage, and the next day, as the townspeople cele-
brated in the plaza, a cloud appeared in the sky, a vision of
Christ on the cross. All of this was captured in paintings on
the walls of the newer church next door. He lingered a long
while before the paintings. A line of half a dozen people
formed in the back, along the last pew by the confessional. A
priest came in and entered the booth, and the line moved.

He found a shaded bench in the square and sat down to
rest.

He could not help addressing Eva; it was a habit he had
never really abandoned. He leaned back against the bench
and closed his eyes. "I liked the paintings. They are very
fine. Do you believe there was a real vision in the sky? Or
was it all an accident of condensation? You would know
such a thing where you are. So tell me, Eva, do you believe
in miracles now?"

He opened his eyes. The real miracle would be Eva, here with him. An itinerary, he knew now, was an act of faith. You believed you would live to see it.

A band of schoolboys in blue uniforms ran in front of him, shouting and tagging one another. An elderly man in a business suit, with a cane, sat on a bench to Riley's right, crossed his hands on the top of the cane, and turned to look at Riley with open curiosity.

Across the square, small clanking buses pulled up, paused a few moments, then pulled away. Riley looked up and saw "Mary of Tears" on one. The driver stepped down to have a smoke. He looked dapper, with a trim mustache, in a crisp white shirt and slim-fitting checked knit trousers. He called out a greeting to a taxi driver, waved at a bus pulling in behind, and stretched. Riley went to ask him about the village.

It was eight miles. The fare was a few centavos. Several passengers got on at the square, peddlers with mostly empty bags and sacks. There were more stops on the way through town, and at each, another rider or two climbed aboard. Outside of town the landscape was brush and rock and dry land. One by one the passengers went to stand by the door and motion toward the side of the road. At places with no apparent landmark, the bus halted and Riley watched through the window as the bus left the passengers behind. They trudged off across the land, toward their ranchos in the distance. From the bus there was no visible sign of population out there. The last four miles were on rough road and took most of the time of the trip. Near the village, Riley saw small tilled fields, plots of corn, and orchards no bigger than the floor plan of his sister's suburban house. Eventually, in the last mile or so, Riley was accompanied only by two women, one carrying a small squealing pig, the other swathed in rebozo and skirts, and hugely pregnant. The pregnant woman got off as the village came into sight and walked toward the slope of a hillside and the wisp of a fire in the distance.

Once the bus entered the village, it seemed impossible that it could navigate the broken and buckled stone street. At one point, Riley was thrown from his seat to the floor, and the woman burst into hoarse laughter, joined by the driver and, in some manner, by the pig. There was nothing for Riley to do but pull himself back to his seat with good humor. The driver parked the bus on a bare—and flat—dirt patch in what appeared to be the center of the village, though there was no plaza in sight. Riley asked the driver when the bus would return to the town. "Six and a half," the driver said. Time enough to look around.

The village was a dusty, unremarkable place, except for the chapel and the ruins of what had been a monastery, built at least two hundred years before. Probably it had been abandoned in the Revolution. The graceful arched door of the chapel was shaded by tall trees. In front was a large courtyard framed by a carved stone railing. On the far side of the chapel, a long stone wall ran one way for what might have been a city block; all Riley could see behind it was the broken roofline of a building. At the chapel steps a vendor was selling souvenirs from an old ice cream cart. He was an old man, missing many teeth, wearing a dark serape and white trousers. His wares were spread out across the top of the cart: laminated holy cards, plastic flowers, wooden rosaries, and curious lengths of crude rope knotted in several places. Riley asked about the ropes.

"For discipline," the old man said.

"How's that?" Riley asked.

The old man laughed, showing his gums. He took one of the ropes and hit himself lightly on one shoulder. "For the penitents," he said. He held one out toward Riley. "For your sins."

Riley declined the little whips and bought a holy card instead. The card was crammed with images: the Virgin, her baby son, angels, several saints and apostles, a pulsing heart in the upper right corner. He tucked it into his wallet. The vendor said, "You have come to see the Virgin, no?" When Riley said he had come for that, the old man said, "They enter close to the earth," and when he again saw Riley's lack of understanding, he fell abruptly to his knees and crawled around from the back of the cart toward the chapel, making his way back and forth like a crippled crab.

Riley intercepted his path and entered the chapel—on his feet.

The statue of the Virgin was unimpressive—two feet tall, a typical Guadalupe, with bruised gilt along the folds of her gown. She stood in a recessed alcove in the back of the chapel. The alcove was festooned with unlit Christmas lights, and in front of the statue were several banks of votive candles and a metal container with a slot for offerings. Riley dropped in a peso.

There was little light in the chapel, and none near the statue, and Riley could not see the Virgin's face very well. Certainly she did not appear to be shedding tears. But who could say? If so many said they had seen them, then surely they had seen something. It was good to think that Mary cried for you. That someone did. It eased the heart, to think that.

He took a taper and lit a candle and said a Hail Mary for his mother, then another for Eva, and another for her dull daughter Bernadette. He bent his head and closed his eyes for a moment to pray. As he opened his eyes again, the Christmas lights suddenly twinkled. In his peripheral vision he caught a glimpse of someone stepping away.

He slid another coin into the offering box. He thought of the señora who had sent him here, and lit yet another candle. Finally, he stuffed some bills into the offering box and lit all the candles, at least a dozen.

He stepped back into a pew to survey the sight of his candles burning. Now he could see that in the front, two women in black rebozos were kneeling on the floor between the pews. They held their arms up and out in front of them; they were saying the rosary together. He could hear the mutter of their voices and the slightest click of the rosary beads as they passed them through their hands.

He felt nostalgic, though he could not think for what.

He thought of the señora's description of the Virgin. "I have no heart's wishes anymore," he whispered. "Please give the nice woman from your village hers."

Back at the vendor's cart, he bought a rosary carved from a rose-colored wood, for his sister, who kept a Mary altar in a cleft under the stairs, off the kitchen; who prayed there every morning before the household woke; who mourned the loss of the Latin Mass, and the hairstyles of her children. She wanted Riley to move to the suburb. Children there needed pets too, she said. They had to drive fifteen miles to find a shop. Everyone spoke English.

The vendor thanked him and said, "How did you like the lights?" When Riley said he had been enchanted, the old man put his hand out and grinned, showing his gums. Riley pressed a coin into his palm.

The hot afternoon light had waned, and there were shadows on the wall that ran up the narrow street away from the chapel. On the other side, a building had been partly demolished, and the rubble lay in heaps in front of it. A long building of brick and stucco, with a single concrete step running its length, had three door openings. The building had once been red and white, with painted signs, but it was sun-bleached and crumbling now. Riley could see men inside; one leaned against the doorway, drinking from a long-necked bottle. Outside, several more lounged against the wall, their hats pushed back, smoking and drinking. Riley realized he was very thirsty, and started toward the men, but he had taken only a few steps when two of the men stepped back inside, and the third went around the corner and out of sight. He lost his courage. Inside, there would be men at the end of a hard day, men who knew one another and would be suspicious of a gringo. What would he say to any of them? What would there be to drink?

He decided to wait by the bus. He leaned against it and looked off across the dirt at the squat buildings opposite, and the alleyway. The air was still and hot, though it would be cool in a little while. He smelled the smoke of cooking fires. Several women entered one of the buildings and came back out in a few minutes, carrying something wrapped in cloth. Suddenly the doughy hot smell of tortillas hit him, like exhaust from a truck, and he realized they were fetching food, and that he was hungry.

"Señor, Señor." A small boy approached him. "You want a beer?"

"Oh yes, I do," Riley said. The boy said he would bring it to him. He took Riley's coin. In a few moments he appeared again, slightly out of breath from his hurry, carrying a small plastic bag twisted shut, with a straw sticking out. He presented it to Riley.

It was his beer.

It wasn't cold, and it wasn't good beer, less so for having been poured into a Baggie, but it slaked his thirst, and he was happy to drink it. The child, maybe six years old, squatted on the ground nearby and watched him drink. He ran over as soon as Riley was done, to ask if he wanted another, and when he said he did not, took the little Baggie and the straw and ran away.

Riley tested the door of the bus and found it pushed open. He climbed the steps and sat a few rows back to wait. He closed his eyes for a moment.

He woke to the rumbling of his stomach, and glanced at his watch. It was seven-thirty. There was no sign of the driver. He looked out the window. There were several children, maybe ten to twelve years old, standing below, staring up at him. When they saw him looking, they laughed and looked at the ground, then up again.

There was nothing to do but go into the bar and ask after the driver. He stepped up and through one of the doors into darkness. "*Perdón, perdón,*" he said. The long narrow room was full of smoke and the acrid smell of sweat. A radio was playing loud cantina music. A fat man wearing a round straw hat asked him how he could help. Riley said he was looking for the driver of the bus. Several men guffawed.

"Already he's drunk," one of them said.

"Gone to his woman," said another.

Riley's stomach turned over. "But the bus—" he stammered. "He said, six-thirty."

"Oh yes, Señor," they told him. "Bright and early in the morning, the driver will be there in his clean shirt."

They turned away again. He half-stumbled back outside. For a moment he felt sick to his stomach, but he made himself take a long, slow breath. So what! he told himself. He misunderstood the time—though what was the driver thinking, to bring him to the village, knowing he could not leave till morning?

He looked around again. There had to be a phone. He would call a taxi to come for him from town. Maybe it would cost him ten dollars, so what? He saw one of the boys sitting in the dirt over by the bus and went to him. As he approached, the youngster jumped up. "Yes sir!" he said.

"I need a taxi," Riley said.

The boy grinned. "No taxi, Señor." Riley glanced around. There were no cars in sight. Far down the street past the chapel, a man walked slowly, bent over beneath the burden of a wooden table.

"From the town," Riley said. "I need to make a call." He put his hand to his ear. "There is a phone office, no?"

"For certain!" the boy said. "Sure, I can take you there."

Riley followed him down the alley between the bar and the tortilla shop, and around one more corner, to the entrance to a tiny room. There were two phones on the wall, with a piece of wood nailed in between them, and at a table, a young woman sat reading a comic book. She wore a white blouse with a deep starched ruffle, and a crucifix that fell partway behind the first button.

"A taxi will come from the town?" Riley asked her.

She glanced up, shrugged, then went back to reading.

"Please, you will call a taxi for me?"

"No, Señor," she said. "I regret it."

"But the phones—" He pointed to the wall.

She shrugged again. "They have not worked since Christmas," she said. "Such a pity."

When he stepped outside again, he looked for the boy and did not see him. A weary man pushed past him, carrying heavy lengths of rope on both shoulders. There was no sign of a place that would let a room.

He made his way back toward the bus. The boy was there with a man. The man held his hat in his hand.

"Señor," he said. "My son has told me you wish to return to the town."

"I do!" Riley said. "Can you help?" He did not think the man looked like someone with an automobile, but you could not know these things.

"Not I, no one, until morning. But you will come with us to my home. It is nothing, Señor, but it is yours tonight, and it is our honor."

"I thought—perhaps—the priest—" Riley said. He pointed toward the chapel.

"There is no priest, Señor," the man said. "The priest comes once a week to say Mass and hear our confessions. He comes from a neighboring village."

Riley said, "I can sleep on the bus."

The man inched his fingers around his hat a quarter turn. "My wife would not sleep all night if you had no supper, Señor. Soon it will be night, and cold, and you will hear the coyotes and feel you are alone." He stepped forward. "Please, honor us with your presence. I am Cayetano, the barber. This is my son Miguelito. My wife is waiting for us. You will stay the night."

Riley followed the child, and the man followed him. He tried not to think of the bed in the hotel, his pajamas, bottled water, a shower. Everything would be there in the morning, when the driver, in his clean shirt, delivered him.

They walked through the village—it did not take long—and beyond it a short distance, past a few skinny chickens and a small pig, to Cayetano's house. It was a low, tin-roofed two-room house. Outside, there were many tin cans attached to the wall and planted with small bright flowers. Inside, the rooms were separated only by a length of fabric, now pulled back to reveal a bed and table, a window with no pane, and a large poster of Jesus with the Sacred Heart. The first room, too, had a bed, a couple of chairs, and a crude cabinet with jars of canned fruit. There were many gilt-framed holy cards—Jesus ascending, a couple of Madonnas, baby Jesus, someone in medieval garb on a draped horse. The front door looked straight through a back door out into the cooking area, where the señora was bustling over a steaming pot, and a grill where tortillas were warming. There seemed to be children everywhere. Cayetano called them to him and lined them up—there were, in fact, seven—and named them. Only two were girls. Each child in turn tucked his or her head and smiled, then looked to the father for permission to run back to the patio and the skirts of their mother, or the freedom of the yard.

Cayetano practiced "Riley" many times to satisfy himself that he was saying it properly. He moved a chair to the center of the room, facing the patio, and bade Riley to sit, then pulled a stool up to sit beside him. Riley could see his wife at her cooking, and the younger girl, seven or eight, helping. Beyond the patio, a boy was practicing with a slingshot, aiming at small bottles and cans lined up on rocks. His father saw him too, and sat taller.

"Your children are handsome," Riley said. "Are they in school?"

Cayetano said, "They are strong children. Already the boys work in the field with their mother." He pointed to the child working on the patio. "The girl works in the house of the mayor, whose wife is sick. Her sister here watches the babies."

A child approached Riley slowly, carrying a toy. He looked to his father, who nodded, and then showed Riley that he had a plastic water pistol. He gave it to Riley to hold. He didn't seem to want anything of Riley, who simply patted the yellow toy and let it lie on his thigh. Cayetano said, "Beto is seven. He is in school. He is very smart, the teacher says. He says Beto could be anything." Cayetano smiled ruefully. "What would that be, do you think? Where would he have to go, and how would he live while he studied?"

Before Riley could respond, the señora called them to eat. Cayetano called for Miguelito to join them. The boy had washed his face and wetted his black hair, smoothed it back from his forehead. "Miguelito works in an orchard," his father said. "He keeps the ground clear. He knows already how to cut the branches back. This is useful, no?"

They sat at a rough table on the patio. By now it was dark, and they ate by the light that spilled from the ceiling bulb inside the house, and candles set in Fanta bottles on the table. The woman and her daughter served them a plate of rice and beans and tortillas, and a plate of fried plantains. The tortillas had been folded and laid out, fanlike, on a plate, sprinkled with cheese and slices of hot pepper. Riley scraped the peppers aside as unobtrusively as he could, but the tortillas were hot where the peppers had lain, and soon he was teary-eyed. In a moment, the daughter brought a bottle of guava soda to the table. *Natural and artificial,* it read. It was crusted with dust. She brought a wet rag and wiped it carefully, then opened it for Riley. It was warm and sticky and unbelievably sweet, but he drank it and thanked her profusely, while Cayetano smiled at him and stuffed his own mouth with more peppers than Riley dreamed possible to eat. The children had gathered at the edge of the patio, but they waited until the men and Miguelito had eaten. Riley wanted to speak: Couldn't they all eat now? Couldn't the señora join them? But he knew it was not for him to say.

They drank coffee that was dipped from a clay jar on the grill. Cayetano offered him a cigarette, and he took it, though he had not smoked a cigarette since he was a boy. It was very strong, and he could not help coughing, which made the other man laugh companionably. Miguelito took a single drag from his father's cigarette, and did not cough at all.

The señora was filling tortillas with rice and beans for the other children, who sat away from the table, on the edge of the patio, or in the dirt.

The two men strolled in the yard for a few moments. Riley could hear loud voices some distance away, a shout, and then laughter. Somewhere a baby was crying. There were radios playing. They stood away from the house, and Cayetano said, "I will show you where to go," and took Riley to an outhouse. He waited for him and then walked with him back through the dark to the house.

Already the supper was cleared. The children were chattering in the house. The curtain between the rooms was drawn. Cayetano's wife and two of the older children arranged a mat on the floor where the chairs had been, and over it threw two rough blankets and a large shawl.

They gave Riley the bed in the front room, though he protested. The two girls slept on the floor. Miguelito and Beto took blankets out onto the patio. The little ones were taken into the other space with their parents. Riley lay down. He heard night insects, something rustling at the edge of the house, then everything quieted. There were murmurs from the other room; Cayetano's wife was praying aloud. He heard Cayetano say, finally, "Amen," and they were quiet. "Listen, Eva," he barely whispered. "Hear where I am."

In the night, something woke him, frightened him. There was a shuffling in the room, the moan of a child. He sat up and looked into the darkness. The moon was a mere sliver, and the light through the door, which was ajar, barely illuminated the sleeping figures. He decided he had been dreaming, and lay back down. He did dream. There were children swimming in a river. They were looking at him. He could see only the top half of their heads; below their noses, they were submerged. The water was murky, still. He couldn't see if the children were happy.

He woke to the sounds of the señora patting tortillas on the patio. It was barely dawn. Cayetano passed through and outside. In the night, the boys had moved inside near their sisters. They all lay in a mound under the shawl.

The two toddlers lay curled alongside Riley, their heads against his hip. Like kittens they were, their closed fists tucked under their chins or the curve of his thigh. He could feel his heart pounding, like that of a man in love. He lay perfectly still, not to disturb the children until the rest of the household rose. He watched until they waked and saw him and blinked in astonishment. One of them gurgled happily and this woke the other. The second child howled.

The strangeness of it. The older girl came and scooped up the child. The other children gathered around and stared at Riley solemnly. When he said, "Good morning, little ones," they scattered, screeching and laughing. A chicken ran through the room, and somewhere, in someone else's yard, a cock crowed.

Poor Ones

IN TECATITLÁN, THE NIGHT HAS TURNED BLACK. The dirt yards still smell faintly of sprinkled water. The square is empty and the streets are quiet. The dog Loza lopes up the Street of San Francisco, trying to catch up with the other dogs who have come down from the hills or out from back alleys to roam. Loza stops to sniff a drunk lying outside the bakery, then wanders on. Above, there is only a sliver of moon, and the hard, bright blink of stars.

In the small barrio above the chapel, where the nicer houses are perched on higher land, electric lights burn in rooms where women are reading sad romantic novels, or writing letters to their children in Mexico City. The baker's wife watches a movie on her new VCR, the sound turned so low (the baker rises at 3:00 A.M.) that she sits on a stool, her face close to the screen, and cries when the heroine is shunned by her lover. Next door, the lawyer's wife, home for a week from their Guadalajara house, rubs cream over her arms and shoulders and thinks of her lover in the city. Her husband, with the dentist, has gone to Don Pedro's to see

the hockey game from Canada, clearly transmitted by satellite dish. Outside Don Pedro's house, in a dark stony place,
Poor One hovers, listening to the rapid announcing and the
laughter and shouts of the men. Don Pedro, called Pete by
many of his male friends, has recently retired back to his village after forty years in Stockton, California, where he was
an electrician and the father of four sons and two daughters,
all grown and successfully established. He has instructed his
kitchen maid to set out a plate for Poor One after supper. He
has left blankets on the edge of the courtyard. The night
watchman is disapproving, but he skirts the sleeping figure
when he makes his rounds. Poor One is harmless, though
foul. Don Pedro has come home a soft American. It is nothing to the watchman, who eats a meal at two in the morning
and catches naps in his hut at the gate.

Don Genaro, grocer and mayor, walks around the
perimeter of the inner courtyard of his apartment building.
He is a descendant of the original owners of the hacienda in
whose Great House deaf children are now housed along
with the American widow, and sometimes, but seldom, Don
Santos, who owns factories in Guadalajara and drives a large
American car. Don Genaro's renters live in one-room apartments furnished with iron cots, toilets, and showers. A few
have American-style stoves; most cook in a communal
kitchen shed along the back of the courtyard. All of them
have gone to bed. Satisfied that all is well, he returns to his
own spacious, well-furnished apartment and carefully combs
his hair and applies a splash of cologne on the back of his
neck. Then he goes into the street.

In another, flat part of town, Consolata Arispe pulls up
the cover over the shoulders of Tía Filomena on the bed in
the alcove off the one room of her adobe house. She kisses
her daughter good night, and goes across the kitchen patio
to her hut. There is no electricity in the hut. She lights a

small lamp. She pours water from a pitcher into a large tin bowl, strips to her waist, and washes. Then she puts on a clean blouse, takes down her hair from braids, and brushes it slowly. She lights candles on the table, fashioned from a fruit crate, that serves as her altar. On the cinderblock wall above, she has hung a length of blue satin, and on it, elaborately framed photographs of Jesus with his pulsing heart, the Virgin ascending into heaven, Pancho Villa, St. Francis. On the tiny table are large candles, tiny jars of herbs, small clay bowls, a sachet box, and color photographs of her son Ruben's green card, his low-rider car, his wife, and their two babies. There is a small statue of Mary.

Consolata burns a small braid of pungent grasses. She kisses the photograph of her son's green card. She turns back the shawl on her bed—a thin mattress on a shelf—then blows out the candles and the lamp and lies down in the dark. She thinks of her dead: her mother, gone in childbirth at thirty. Her father, a mule driver, killed by a bandit on the road. Three sisters, two brothers, all dead before adulthood. Her son Angel, who went on a government bus to Mexico as part of an arranged crowd for a demonstration, and was crushed by an army truck in the street. Her sons' father, Javier, a peddler who took her from her village at fourteen, and died in a brawl when she was twenty. Her infant daughter Maria, who never took a breath of air. She remembers, as one remembers a wind through trees, or the smell of oranges in a grove. As one remembers cloth, or stones, a flood, the calls of birds.

Don Genaro, at the corner one street over from Consolata's house, turns into the path of the priest, Luis Bernal.

"Out for a walk, Don Genaro?" the priest says.

What can the grocer say but yes? They stand on the corner for a few moments and chat about the upcoming fiesta. Don Genaro is responsible for much of the planning for contests and events, although this year, thankfully, he has the able assistance of Don Pedro. The fiesta honors the Virgin with the lighting of hundreds of candles, blessed by the padre. "Yes, yes, it is proceeding," Don Genaro says, as patiently as he can.

Father Bernal turns back in the direction from which he has come, toward the church and his small house. "See you at Mass, Don Genaro," he says. The priest goes only where he is invited, and, of course, to all public events. There are those who despise him. The schoolmaster steps away to let him pass. The baker turns his back to him, though his wife prays daily and sobs to her husband that the priest is a good man. No one can find more to say against him than that he walks about late at night.

"Till Sunday, Father," Don Genaro says. "Good night." He hurries, but when he reaches Consolata's house, he sees that there is no light in her hut. He stands in the street outside the house. Through the window he sees Consolata's daughter Divina at a table under the hanging bulb, with a book. As he watches, she rises and comes to the window and peers outside. She crosses her arms across her breasts, and rocks back and forth gently. He steps back into shadow. She pulls a cloth across the opening and shuts out his gaze.

He starts up the hill to Don Pedro's and the company of men.

Outside the church, the American woman Charlotte Amory sits on a bench. Father Bernal sits down beside her, and when she slips her hand into his, he clasps it for a moment.

"It's been twelve years today," Charlotte says. "I've thought about her all day long. I woke before dawn."

"A long day, then," Father says.

"I went over to the school and helped with lunch."

"A good deed, then," Father says.

"It was for me, you understand."

"Most good deeds are for the doer. That doesn't keep them from being good."

"I thought it would get easier," she says. "I thought you were talking it over with God for me. Because I have no words, you know. Not for this."

"And it hasn't?"

"The thought of her isn't constant, so the pain isn't constant, either. But when it comes, it's the same. Like a gale. I can't shut the door on it."

"Grief takes its own time. There is a reason for it. Maybe, if you could turn to it, you would be filled. I feel the emptiness in you. It's like a draft from a cave. It's a wind I know, Charlotte. Sorrow is the part of memory that holds you, and grieving is the part that goes on from sorrow." He smiled. "The English—have I mixed things up?"

Charlotte runs her hand through her hair and holds her head at the back. Her arm crosses her face. "I'll never forget. God, I can't do that. But will it ever ease? Just that? A matter of degree? Something dulled?"

"All things ease, Charlotte. The supplicant prays when there is no answer, because he knows. All things ease."

"My mother wrote. 'I never thought you'd stay so long,' she says. She reminds me that Wimberly, too, is a village. 'I've turned a corner,' she says. 'I see myself as an old woman.' She would like for me to be there. There's some logic to it."

"She means to comfort you."

"She doesn't want to be old alone."

"Does anyone?"

She touches his hand again. "Saturday. Come to supper, please. It will help. I will cook it myself." She feels his refusal forming. He arranges never to be alone with her, except here, in the chapel environs. "I am asking Tom Riley. He remembers you."

"I'll come," he says. "I've read all the books you lent me. Are there more?"

"A fresh box from a friend in New York. Remainders, they're called. Books that didn't do well. Sometimes they're the best ones. I don't think I have the taste of most readers."

"Choose a few for me."

"Luis—" She pronounces his name *Lou-ee,* with the familiarity of a friend. "I didn't need to leave them. I told myself lies. A drama I thought I had to play out for myself. I don't remember anymore what I thought was so wrong. I don't remember what I thought I wanted. Not really."

"It was a long time ago. You were young."

"She was a baby. I left her. She died. It's not much of a plot. The events are too strung out, too lacking in causality. But oh, the guilt of the protagonist! Oh, the absence of a hero!"

"You couldn't have changed God's will. You didn't make the accident happen. It could have happened if you were there. And you have suffered, too. There is no way for you to mend the tear between you and your child. There never will be. But only you are in pain. She is with God. She is with the mother of us all."

"I didn't have anything to give. Not then. Not ever, really. Her father will never understand that, but I think, over time, my mother has come to. I am who I have become, and she couldn't have made me better. I'm not a good person, Luis."

"That's not so. You are a friend to many. You give us important things. Affection for our memories. Faith in our dreams."

"You say 'us,' Luis. Do you include yourself?"

The priest stands up. "I have lived a long time on the strength of the memory of faith, and faith that faith will come again, and if that is not a dream, what is?"

Charlotte whistles sharply and calls out, "Loza! Come

home! Loza!" The dog comes running clumsily down the street toward her. "Good night, then," she says to the priest.

"I pray for her. I pray for you."

"I don't mind."

In the chapel, the priest kneels with his face in his hands. His soul, like the stripped church, is bare. The bell was stolen in the Revolution. On the walls there were once paintings of the Sacraments. Only these remain: Baptism, Marriage, and Extreme Unction. The alcoves hold simple statues, and the offerings of flowers and candles in jars and bottles and cracked dishes.

Tía Filomena sleeps. Her hands are crossed on her stomach. Her fingers twitch as she dreams of doilies. Between her shoulder and the wall she has tucked her prize possession, an alarm clock, which is never wound.

Divina sits at the table in the middle of the room. There are so many doilies on the wall, a first glance might see them as a design. Behind her, though, on the part of the wall she claims as her own, she has tacked up pictures from magazines given her by the American: fashion models and elegant houses, photographs of tables laid with china and folded napkins. She sits under the naked bulb, her radio playing low, and hums softly. She nibbles at slices of squash candy dipped in honey. Slowly, in a whisper, she reads from a tattered copy of *The Sun Also Rises*.

Dispatches

THE CLERK GREETS RILEY'S RETURN with a stack of messages. *Your sister called.* There are three of those, the last only an hour earlier. There is a note from Joe Flaxman about the boxing bout in the city: *A couple of us are driving over Friday night, you better come.* That's tonight. He looks around the lobby, then steps back, away from the line of view of the residents out by the pool. If he doesn't see Flaxman, he won't even have to decline. Another note is from Flaxman's wife, Brenda. *Never mind the brutal stuff, Tom. There's a party. See me!* And two little hearts. A second note from Brenda. *There's someone I want you to meet.* And one from Charlotte. *Save Saturday. I'll pick you up at four.*

Goodness, he thinks. Go away and find out how many people know you're gone!

He goes down the avenue and around the corner to the long-distance telephone office. There are three booths along the wall. All are occupied when he enters the room. *At least these work,* he thinks.

When it is his turn, he calls the shop and speaks with his

assistant, Dora. "Don't worry about anything," she tells him. "My nephew Bobby comes in and helps with the cages. Things are slow. We had four inches of snow yesterday. You are in the right place there! If I were you, I wouldn't come home till we have spring. Till we have spring three days in a row, just to be sure."

"If you get tired, shut it up for a day or two," he tells her.

"And then what would I do, Riley? You don't worry, okay?"

Next he calls his house. The rings go on and on; just as he would hang up, Derek answers, all out of breath.

"I was shoveling, Uncle Riley. Jeez, we had snow yesterday—"

"I heard."

"You talked to Mom?"

"I called the shop."

"Are you having a good time?"

"It's beautiful here. Derek. How's Sweetly? How's Goldie? You're giving them lots of pats, are you?" He misses his dogs; he feels it like a poke in the chest.

"Uncle Riley, they sleep on my bed. My friends slip them cookies. Don't worry."

"Everybody says that."

"Huh?"

"I better call Margaret."

"Yeah, well, good luck. She's all upset."

"Because I'm gone?"

"That doesn't help. But no, it's me."

"What've you done?"

"Don't let me spoil her fun. She can tell you. Besides, I know what you'll say."

"What's that?"

"You'll say it's my business. You'll say a young man with no obligations can choose whatever he wants for himself.

It's when people depend on you that that changes."

"How do you know all that?"

"Jeez, Uncle Riley. You lived with Grandma till she dropped over. You think I didn't watch that? You think I didn't notice?"

"You be good to your mom."

"Sure."

"You rub Goldie's belly for me. Comb Sweetly's ears."

"You got it."

He takes the little warning of his sister's mood. He can see her in the kitchen, leaning against the china hutch, tapping her foot. People not behaving. The weather dropping on her. Her brother off someplace warm, where you can't drink the water and they say Mass in Spanish. But what can she do? He's far away, at the other end of a phone line. It makes him smile.

"I was just about frantic, Tom," she says.

"Everything's fine."

"Maybe there it is. Here it's not so fine. Richard had to let an employee go this week. She was stealing petty cash. He didn't call the police. Stupid, isn't it?"

He chooses to assume she's talking about the thief. "Pretty desperate." Richard's a good fellow. Benign, even. All these years, he's gone about his life, liking his work, loving his family, enjoying his wife's obsessions as if they were goldfish in a tank.

"Annie's missed two days of school with a bad cold."

"Give her my love. Not a kiss, though. Everybody needs you on your feet, Margie."

"Don't call me Margie, Tom."

"Call me Riley."

"Oh, honestly. Aren't you about done with this?"

"My vacation? It's only been a week. I'm just getting my bearings."

"You know the thrift shop is going to let its lease go?"

"I didn't know that." The thrift shop is next door to the pet store in the building owned by Riley.

"You could expand."

"I don't know, Margaret."

"You've been saying you'd expand if that space became available. You've said it for years. A bicycle shop. Coffee beans."

"Expanding was Eva's idea. I haven't thought about it lately."

"You could remodel and lease the whole building out. You could move your shop out here."

"This is pretty expensive, Margaret. Talking about this from Mexico."

"You won't believe what Derek's done."

"Is it legal?"

"Legal? Of course it's legal. Tom, he's dropped out of college. He never even registered for this semester, but I didn't know till this week."

"There's more, isn't there? About what he's doing?"

There's an edge of hysteria in her voice. Her son, out of control. He is actually eager to hear.

"He's enrolled in hairdressing school. Derek is going to be a hairdresser."

"You don't say. Margie, I've got to go. There are people in line."

"Can't you call me from the hotel?"

"No phones in the room."

"What kind of hotel—"

"Hey. He's a great kid. He'll be a great hairdresser. I'll let him cut my hair, promise."

"That's what he said. 'Uncle Riley'll let me practice on him.' Richard laughed."

"It is pretty funny. 'Bye, Margie. Love."

"Tom—"

He leaves the booth laughing.

At the Patio, the iron gate is partway down. The tables and chairs are inside, in stacks.

"Señor, Señor, closed," the señora calls from behind the counter. She wags her finger back and forth. "No more today, come tomorrow."

"Till tomorrow, then," he answers.

"Oh, Señor, it's you. Come in, I can find you something. A cold drink?"

"No, no. I only wanted to say hello. I'll come tomorrow for lunch."

"Yes. I'll make a special dish. A pork mole, with chiles *anchos* and plantain. Not too hot."

"Don't change your recipe for me. I'll try hot. Señora, I came to tell you I went to your village. It was very special, as it turned out."

"Sit down, you're here now. Tell me about my village." From the cold case behind her she takes a beer and sets it on the counter. "Did the Virgin weep?"

He takes a long cool drink. He feels it gush in his head. The señora's hair is damp at the temples and above her forehead. *How hard she works,* he thinks. *How kind she is.*

He had not thought of her as pretty, but now he sees how fine is the arch of her brows, how clear and proud her gaze.

He tells her, "I lit a votive candle for you in the chapel, Señora."

"You are too kind. And did you see the tears?"

"I didn't see them spill. But I saw the glaze they leave on her cheeks." He is so pleased to see her smile, he forgets it is a lie. A small, white lie; it was dim in the chapel. He was tired.

"Señor—" She speaks softly, and points to his face. He puts his fingers up to his cheeks. He feels the tears that have spilled and spread.

"My wife—" His voice breaks. The emotions are as sudden and irrepressible as the cough after Cayetano's cigarette, the sting of his eyes after a bite of chiles. "She went so many places—"

"But not to the village of Mary of Tears," the señora says. *She understands,* he thinks.

"She is dead."

"You lit a candle for her, then. Mary will help your heart."

"I don't know. I lit many candles, but maybe they were all for me."

He takes another drink, and reaches in his pocket for a coin.

"No, no, Señor. It is nothing."

"Thank you."

"Tomorrow. You will come for my mole?"

"I will come early, to take the first taste."

"Come earlier still, Señor, and I will show you how I make it."

He starts to go, then thinks to say, "I spent the night. It was a misunderstanding with the bus. I had no way to return to the town. I stayed with the family of the barber, Cayetano."

"You had an adventure then, Señor."

"Till tomorrow," he says. The thought of it makes him happy.

On the street he hears his name. "Riley, wait up! I'm so glad I saw you." It is Brenda Flaxman, vivid in a yellow sundress and a big straw hat. She has the sunny smile, the open posture of a forties movie star. She's carrying a straw purse the size of a grocery bag. She shifts it to her other shoulder and takes his arm. It's a nice feeling.

A Ride to
the Suburbs

THE SOMEONE RILEY HAD TO MEET was a widow named Renata
Bennett. She gave Riley and Brenda a ride to the party,
which was up in the hills above Lago, a couple miles' drive.
As they got to her car, a nice green Olds, he admired it, and
she offered to let him drive. "I don't know where we're
going," he reminded her, and she said, "Carl couldn't bear to
ride in a car a woman was driving," and got in the driver's
seat herself.

The house was one of a whole development of American-style homes, beautifully landscaped, some of them with
high fences. Renata said they had their own water system,
you could drink water right from the tap. They had their
own security patrol. They had a housing board; you couldn't
sell to just anybody, you had to have approval. She lived up
here, too, she said, but her house was going on the market
sometime soon. However long it took to sell, that was how
long she had to figure out what to do next. "I love Lago," she

said, "but it's no fun being single here." He wondered how long Carl had been dead.

Once he was in the house, he felt he might have been in a suburb of Chicago instead of Lago de Luz, except that it was a lot warmer and the grounds were lush and the air soft and fragrant. The house was built on several levels against a hillside, with a pool and pool house. Around the pool were tables and chairs and a huge gas-fired barbecue. The house was owned by a retired army officer and there were photographs of him with Bob Hope and Ronald Reagan and lesser dignitaries. In fact, the walls were just about covered with photos—Colonel Reed with a marlin, Mrs. Reed with her children, their children with their spouses and their children, and dogs and horses and graduations and weddings.

His sister would have loved it.

He met all kinds of people and hardly remembered a name. Les and Kitty, from the Posada, were there, acceptable candidates for a house, though they were talking about Alamos, over by the west coast, a silver mining town, less developed and closer to the border.

Riley found a chair by the pool and a big, pretty retriever stretched out beside it. He reached down to scratch its belly and missed Goldie terribly for a moment, and then Brenda came and sat down beside him.

"A crowd's a crowd, wherever you go," she said. Her pretty silk blouse curved over her breasts and fell softly to her hips.

"They seem like nice people."

"They are. Some of the ancient ones will go home early and it'll be more fun. You'll see. Do you dance?"

He winced. "I met my wife at a dance. It was a party for a christening."

"So you do dance," Brenda said matter-of-factly. "Consider

my card marked first." She got back up. "The buffet's out, come and eat. Renata's dying to talk to you."

"I don't know, Brenda—"

"It's just what you need. She's a few years older than you, does that bother you? She's thin and fit. Close your eyes, you'll never know." She laughed. "I can get a ride with somebody."

"If you mean what I think you do, we don't know each other well enough to talk like this."

She laughed again. "Somebody needs to talk to you, Riley. You're a good-looking fellow, and as far as I can see, you don't drink, so you'll still be awake when the party's over. If I weren't sworn to be faithful this time around, I'd chew on your ear myself."

He was blushing a deep, hot scarlet. He didn't know how to make her stop.

"Din-din!" he heard someone shout. "Come and get it."

They walked to the buffet together. "I'm a pretty straight fellow," he told her. "I don't know what Joe told you."

"Joe told me to keep my hands off," she said, but he thought she was teasing.

He took his plate into the house and found a seat on one of the couches, near several couples who introduced themselves as neighbors. The food was good, typical American barbecue fare, except for the Mexican-style dips and chips and the punch bowl of margaritas. He felt better as he ate. Surrounded by couples, he felt friendly. When they asked him what he'd been up to, he found he felt like talking. He told them about the museum and the miracle paintings he'd seen, and how he'd like to see some petroglyphs, and they told him about the butterflies and a mountain town where they had a rodeo in February, and he relaxed. He excused himself and got a margarita. He took his time, moving along the walls, looking at photos, sipping his drink. Some men were arguing, in a friendly way, about the trade agreement. One of them thought poor Mexicans would be having televisions and vacations soon, it would change everything, and the other man said that kind of wishful thinking just covered up corporate greed and government foolishness, and they said they'd have to settle it in a game of tennis soon, and they clapped one another on the back. He made a right turn over by the sound system, and heard a woman with hair like a poodle telling somebody her husband's bladder tumors had turned out to be benign.

When he got back to his seat, which the others had saved for him, somebody was talking about the pyramids at Tula. He leaned forward eagerly. "I could see those, couldn't I?" he asked. "I mean, it's not like trying to get to Egypt." One of the couples had been to Egypt, had ridden camels and everything. "You can't compare Mayan and Egyptian pyramids," the woman said. "Apples and oranges." She said they'd gone when the travel agent said it would be the best weather, but she'd still suffered from the heat. "What I'll never forget," she said, "was how tiny the passages were inside. I didn't go in. Mostly, you couldn't. But you could see how explorers had to squeeze in, lordy!"

"Or grave robbers," someone commented.

"I don't see how anything could be more impressive than Chichén Itzá," a tall, thin man said. Riley remembered his name, because it was the same as his brother-in-law's, Richard. "The power of those massive monuments rising out of jungle, it's something to behold."

"I guess it's whether you like your temples wet or dry," his wife said gaily, patting her husband's knee. "I'd love a drink, honey," she said, ending a conversation Riley might have enjoyed.

In the lull, he told them about spending the night in the

village of Mary of Tears, of how nice the family had been to him. He could tell they were aghast. One of the women wanted to know what the ceiling of the house had been made of, and he couldn't remember. He probably had never looked. She was afraid of scorpions.

He told them about waking up to the sight of all those children peering at him like the curiosity he surely was. "I wish I'd had my camera with me," he said.

"Those village children are like people from the middle ages," Richard's wife said. She had her margarita by then. "Richard and I had some of them with us one year. We were living in Kansas City. Something through the church. They brought these peasant children up to us. You'd think they were from the moon. They couldn't get the hang of it. I'd go in the bathroom and they would have used the toilet and then piled the paper up on the floor. I told them—well, I'm sorry, what a discussion, but I was glad to see them go. They got sick, eating my food. They got out of bed at night and wandered outside. I told the program people, you've got to screen these kids better."

Richard put his arm around her. "Twila's as generous as the day is long, but those kids got to her." He rubbed her shoulder. "I told her, that's the whole point. Show them another way to live. But then, when you think about it, what's the point of that? Make them want things they can't have."

Riley excused himself and went outside, past the pool, to the edge of the light. He was standing in a little olive grove. He was gulping air. When someone touched his shoulder, he jumped. It was the widow, Renata.

"They're old bores," she said softly. She stood very near him. They had a view of Lago. The air was almost cold. Renata had draped a shawl around her shoulders. "We were here eleven years. I'm going to make a lot of money on my house. I'm thinking of Oklahoma. That's where I'm from. Sell a house in Lago, you can save a bundle, moving back to Lawton. What do you think they'd make of me in Lawton?"

"I've never been to Oklahoma," he said.

She tucked her arm around his, but there was nothing cozy about her voice. "I know your type. You speak Spanish, don't you? Don't mind traveling on a bus. Do you have a backpack, too? There are other Americans here you'd like better. Watch, you'll see them in the cafes. They have their own little world. Or maybe what you ought to do is meet a Mexican woman. Someone with an education."

He thought she sounded bitter. What had he done?

"I don't know how I've offended you," he said. "But I'm sorry." She was standing very close. He smelled her perfume, and her hair. He pulled away gently.

"How embarrassing, for both of us," she said.

"I'm still—connected—to my wife." His throat was so tight he felt strangled.

"Now that's what I call foolish," Renata said. "In case you haven't noticed, you and I are alive, and they are not."

He didn't know how long he stood there, looking at the lights of Lago. He could see twinkles out on the lake itself. There was an island or two out there.

In a while, Brenda found him. "I've got us a ride," she said. She patted his back, as if in consolation. The queer thing about it was, he liked her touch. He wished he could put his arms around her. It wasn't like what Renata wanted—if he'd understood her right—it was just this awful loneliness. He kept thinking about Cayetano waking up in the morning to a house full of children.

"I lived with my mother until she died," he told her. "Then there was Eva. It was such a relief to marry. I don't like being alone. I'm a lost man without a woman."

"What can I say?" Brenda said. She didn't sound all that sympathetic.

"I suppose I should let my sister fix me up." As soon as he said it, he knew he didn't mean it. For one thing, he didn't think his sister really knew him. He had always been her little brother, as if that defined him.

"Come on, Riley," Brenda said. "I'm every bit as bored as you are, let's nudge Les and Kitty along."

He wanted to be a good sport. What had he come to a party for, if he was going to be melancholy?

"There'll be all kinds of city people in town," he said. "There'll be bands in the plaza, and down by the lake. Would you let me buy you a drink? Would you want to walk around a while? I think I'd like that. Being in Mexico, since that's where I am."

"It's early," she said. "I might want two drinks. I might want to dance. We won't tell Joe."

She wasn't angry. He was relieved. "Whatever you say," he said. "Within reason. I'm Catholic, remember." She giggled.

A
Night Visit

TWICE, OVER THE YEARS, Consolata Arispe had come to my door. Both times, it was to say that Divina was ill and could not come to pose for me. Both times, I invited her in, and she refused. She had never asked me about the pictures I was making of her daughter. Yet when I saw her, as I often did, at her cafe, she was warm and gracious. When I said to her, putting my hand on hers, "Can we be friends? Charlotte and Consolata? It would be so nice for me," she said, "You are good to my daughter," and I took that to be yes.

I decided that the Great House made her uncomfortable. Certainly the house was impressively grand, once you were past the crumbling walls and the front gate, and the long walk bordered by bougainvillea and pots of palms. The roof of the overhang was tiled in red. The front door was of carved wood, a beautiful piece Elias had bought from a master craftsman in Guadalajara. The entrance foyer was laid with blue ceramic tile.

She stood in the door and pulled her rebozo tighter around her shoulders.

"Come in, please," I said, and she stepped inside. "What can I do for you?"

"It's late," she said. "But Divina said you would be awake."

"For hours yet."

"I wish to speak to you."

"It is my pleasure."

"Divina said you write down stories."

"Sometimes." *Oh, no,* I thought, as I had the first time I saw her daughter. *What does she want from me?* I imagined her telling me her life like a tourist back from a journey. *Here is what I saw. Here are the stops I made.* I had recently read an account of a woman's life in another part of Mexico. The writer had spent months and months taping the story. She was an anthropologist, with an interest in such things.

"I want to tell you something."

"Yes, Consolata, of course. Let's go to my room. We will be comfortable there."

As I led her along the veranda, past the kitchen and dining area, past Elias's rooms, to the corner where I lived, I wondered what she would expect of me. Did she think I would tape what she had to say? Was I to take notes? Did she think it would be published in a book? My temples were pounding. I had been looking through the books my friend had sent me from New York. I had been looking for something I could read and enjoy without being jealous.

I motioned for her to sit at the table by my window. I heard the night watchman padding by. She took no notice, but arranged herself in the chair and loosened her shawl. Usually when I saw her she was wearing cheap factory-made clothes, but tonight she wore an embroidered blouse and a long, dark skirt. She had wound her hair on her head in a coil.

"Tell me, then," I said, as I sat across from her. There were books on the table, a school tablet and pens. I would wait and take my cue from her, I thought. I would have to see what it was she expected.

I realized, as if someone had announced it, that I had taken much pleasure in imagining the lives of the villagers, of Consolata, in fact, whose past was full of contradictions. Husbands who may not have been husbands at all. Deaths that may have been abandonments. I had thought myself curious, and I had speculated many times, but I saw immediately that I had never really wanted to know. I admired her—I knew she had once sold fruit and candies on the street, that somehow—with the help of her migrant son, I assumed—she had pulled herself along to where she was now, with her small cafe. I felt affection for her daughter. But I didn't really want to know them; I didn't want to be involved.

I didn't want anyone to ask anything of me.

"The gringo at the Patio," she said, in the flat tone of an announcement.

"I don't understand."

"He came with you. He has come again since then, alone."

"Do you mean Mr. Riley? Thomas Riley?"

"Señor Riley. Yes. He told me today that his wife is dead. That is Señor Riley, no?"

"She has been dead more than a year, I believe," I said.

"He lives far away?"

"In the middle of the United States, which is a big country, like Mexico."

"How far, on the bus?"

"Maybe a week."

"On a plane?"

"It is nothing on a plane. Half a day."

"He is Catholic?"

"I'm sure he said he was."

"He has a good temper. Not like Mexican men."

"I have known kind Mexican men," I said, and regretted my arrogance. "Yes," I quickly added. "He is a nice man."

"Divina says you have been in books."

"One book. A long time ago."

"I want to tell you something."

"Yes, you said. Should I take notes? About your life?" I suppressed my desire to yawn.

"No, not my life." She giggled, suddenly shy. Then, all business again, she said, "It is about a village in the heart of a grand city."

I took up my pen and pulled the pad toward me.

She put her hand on the paper. "Listen," she said, and I put the pen back down. She said, "Neighbors cluster around courtyards, passing *tomatillos* and roses back and forth on summer mornings. In the streets, ice cream vendors call out, and children riding stick horses pull up to ask for scoops of mango ice. Old women rock on porches and sleep and wake and sleep. The young women paint the rooms of their houses in blues and yellows and greens, like bird wings." She took a deep breath.

"Consolata, from where does this story come?"

"I've dreamed it," she said. She leaned toward me, spoke in a deep voice. "Their children come home from school and scold them. 'Speak English, Mami,' they say." She closed her eyes and leaned back in her chair. I was shaken by her talk.

"Is that the story, then?" I asked in a few moments.

"No," she said. "That is only the dream. I don't know how to tell a story."

"Like a fairy tale, perhaps," I said. I thought I understood what she wanted, and it made me shiver. I did want to write it down, though, all of it. As soon as she left, I would.

"How does a fairy tale begin?" she asked.

"Like this: Once upon a time."

"Ah. Once upon a time. Once upon a time, a man traveled to a far place to look for what he had lost." She looked at me so intensely, I thought I could feel the light from her eyes.

"Yes, yes," I said.

"He was a timid man with a good heart."

"Go on."

"I'm not sure. Here it stops. Charlotte—" She put her hands on the table in front of her, like a fortune-teller. "A man can be awakened. A man can become brave."

"I have heard it said, Consolata, that you have special powers."

"Only as a woman knows things," she said. "Though it doesn't hurt to burn herbs."

"I think I understand," I said. "You want me to help you write your story, that's it, isn't it?"

"My husband was a peddler. He came through my village with his mule and his cart. The third time, he told me he lived by a lake. I had never tasted fish. I didn't know what was out there, but I wasn't afraid. I had been waiting. I was eager."

"I bet you were," I said.

"I knew it was right to go, because the way for it came along," she said. "He came, and I saw that was to be my way."

"I do understand," I said. "You know what happens, but you need help with the beginning. The early part, when no one sees the happy ending. Am I right?"

She crossed herself. "God gives us ideas like seeds. He means for them to grow."

A Lap
for a Dog

"WHAT WOULD YOU SAY," Riley asked, "if I told you I think I'm in love?"

We were in my kitchen late in the afternoon. Riley was peeling potatoes from my garden while I dredged chicken pieces in flour and placed them just so in a clay roaster. I pressed a thumb deep into the flesh of a thigh, but gave away nothing of my surprise.

"I'd say you are a lucky man," I replied, "and I'd say, 'Who's the lucky woman?'"

He laughed. "It's not a woman, Charlotte, it's a place. I'm in love with the whole region! Just look out there, what a glorious afternoon."

From where he sat, his back to the veranda, he would see hills out the kitchen windows. Just above the line of brush visible to us, there were little plots where families lived and raised corn and beans. The gardener lived up there somewhere; I had watched him many times, trudging off in the dusk.

Riley pared the last of the potatoes, so that the peeling wound around in one long strip. He put the knife down and showed me the potato like a prize. As if it proved his point.

"Thank you," I said.

I slid the pot of chicken into the oven. "I'm assuming you're getting plenty of Mexican food while you're here," I said. "So I'm sticking with one of my old standbys. Chicken in a wine sauce, and vegetables. Like your mother used to make, I suppose."

"My mother thought all chickens were born to be boiled," he said. He was in a cheery mood. I was glad to see it. In some funny way, he had reminded me of Elias, who was always melancholy, but generous in spirit at the same time.

He went on. "This morning I went for my walk and stopped in the square for coffee. There was a woman selling fortune cookies out of a bird cage. She was all wrapped up like in a rebozo, but it was a beach towel. You paid her a few cents, and her little parakeet pecked at a cookie. Inside the cookie the bird chose your fortune for you. Mine said, 'Ask for cheese, and they give you a bone.' I spent the whole day pondering that one. I thought, Isn't it the truth, though?"

I made a guess. "You never get what you ask for?"

"I was thinking, you get stuck on what you think you need, and somebody else sees it better from outside you." He shrugged.

I took the bowl of potatoes, broke off sprigs of rosemary from the pot on the windowsill and crushed them over the potatoes, then slid them into the oven.

Riley appeared to be quite comfortable sitting there as I worked. In fact, I was enjoying the scene myself, preparing the food, anticipating the meal in the company of friends. I wiped the counter where I'd been working and washed my hands. I poured us each a glass of red wine, and sat down across from him.

"Do you ever wonder when it was you decided to be who you are?" he asked.

"I'm not sure what you mean," I said, though I had a good idea.

"Once I wanted to be a monk, and instead I bought a pet store. I told myself it was a vocation. People need small creatures around them in a city."

"Do you have a dog?"

"Two of them. Goldie's old. She was a mistake off of my sister's prize lab. She follows me from room to room when I'm home. Gets up on the end of the bed when I'm not looking. Then there's Sweetly, she's my Papillon. Not a dog I'd have thought to have, to tell you the truth. Expensive. She's the only one I've ever had in the store. Just not my neighborhood. But I brought my wife in one night. She wasn't my wife yet, we'd only just met. I wanted her to see what I did. And this little pup, she must have weighed a pound and a half, you could hold her in your one hand. Eva picked her up and cooed over her, rubbed her face against her. She had great big ears. Oh, the dog, I mean!"

He laughed at his own joke. His cheeks were bright with color. "Well, she put her back in the cage and we went on about our business, but later, when I'd taken Eva home, I went back and got the dog and took her to my house. I took her right in bed, she was such a little bitty thing. I think I knew right then I wanted to marry Eva. It scared me half to death, thinking I'd come up with an idea that didn't have a chance, so the dog was a comfort and a good luck charm, all in one."

"And then you had the dog and the wife both."

"The dog was a charm, that was it. And now she's still a

comfort. I come home in the evening and she's up on the windowsill by the back porch watching for me."

A wistfulness played across his face. *Uh-oh,* I thought. I'd been enjoying his good spirits.

"Who's looking after your dogs now?"

"My nephew's in the house. He's been living with me a while."

I sipped my wine. He was blushing. "So now you know how to wind me up," he said. "Ask about a dog."

I laughed. "You're very good company, Riley. Here, let's sit out on the veranda."

Across the gardens, children from the residence were playing ball. I could hear the thump of the ball, and now and then the odd sounds of the children's calls. Mostly they were out of sight, though. The littlest ones would be at dinner, and then to bed. Sometimes in the evening I sat at my window and watched the lights go out, one by one, down the length of the wing. Did someone go around and kiss the little ones good night? I'd wondered. Did they miss their parents? They were lucky, I was sure, to have this education. But it wasn't home. It wasn't Mama.

"How much longer will you stay?" I asked Riley.

"I thought I'd stay two weeks, but the first has gone by in a flash. I'm not ready to shovel snow yet. Maybe a couple weeks more," he said. "It's driving my sister crazy. I'm coming back, too, I've already decided that. There are a lot of places around here I'd like to see. What about you? Do you know how long you'll stay? Do you think of this as home?"

"My," I said. "Where do I start?"

He grinned. "It *is* your turn, you know."

"I've been here four years. It's never been a conscious decision, to stay this long or that long. I haven't had a reason to leave, that's all. My mother would like for me to spend some time with her in Texas. She says the motel is too much for her to run alone. And I think about looking for a teaching position somewhere. Or maybe tackling another book. But I get up every day and I don't see why I have to think about any of it yet. It doesn't take much here. I like it."

"Have you got friends here, in the village?"

"Everyone is the soul of politeness. 'Good day, Señora,' they say. 'Good health to you, Señora.' They never show what they think of anything, not to me. I could live here a hundred years and still be a stranger. But I don't mind. I know I'm visiting. And they don't mind, either."

"There's Father Bernal. Have you gotten to know him well?"

"I see him every day, at least in passing. But he's a mystery. He is very private. Of course, he's the only priest I've ever known. Maybe they're all like that."

"You'd think he'd be in a city."

"I don't know if anyone thinks of it: Why is this educated European priest here, in little Tecatitlán? If they do wonder, I suppose they assume it's some kind of penance."

"From his superiors?"

"Sure. Maybe he was too proud, and they sent him here to teach him humility. Maybe he lifted his skirts somewhere, and Tecatitlán is his cross."

Riley was staring at his lap.

"A joke, Riley. Of course. I know very little about Luis. He's from Spain. He studied in Dublin. I think he spent time in the Vatican. Why he's here is anybody's guess. I think it suits him, too. Some of us, well, we just end up here. As far as that goes, half the people in this village come from someplace else. When the haciendas were broken up, people scattered, some came here for land from other villages, and the ones here went who knows where. Musical *ejidos*. The village has been here for hundreds of years, but a lot of the people are newcomers, just a couple of generations. Like Consolata. Her children were born here."

"Consolata?" asked Riley.

"The woman who runs the Patio."

"I showed her my fortune from the cookie this morning. She said they buy them from a vendor who comes every month from the city. I said, 'So they mean nothing?' and she said, 'Fortunes all come from somewhere,' which I took to mean they might have meaning. They're superstitious, aren't they? Gosh, I sound like a terrible gringo, don't I?"

"Superstitious. Fatalistic. So they say. I'll tell you something about Consolata. About Indian women. They survive. And they believe in miracles. Do you believe in miracles?"

"I don't know. I think—they're probably things I don't know about. Things I haven't seen yet. My wife, Eva, believed in them. She went all over the world to places where there had been apparitions and wonders. I want to believe. I'd be happy with some very small miracle. It wouldn't have to be my own."

"Here, a miracle isn't a miracle as we know it. A miracle is the thing that's truly real. God doesn't so much make it happen as reveal it."

"You sound like it's something you've been thinking about," he said.

"Everybody can use a good miracle."

I took him out to the garden. Loza roused himself from a shady spot under a coffee bush and ambled along behind us. When we went back to the veranda, he settled down by Riley's chair. I poured more wine for us.

"This is good," Riley said. "Not that I know that much about wine."

Elias had given a case to me. "It was a gift," I told Riley.

I held my glass up. "To your good spirits, Riley," I said.

He grinned and clicked his glass against mine. "Should we wait on Luis?"

"Luis will be a while. He has confessions to hear."

"I don't usually talk so much," Riley said. He reached down to scratch Loza's ears.

Then he raised his glass. "To new friends," he said.

"And the possibility of little miracles," I added.

Father Bernal isn't wearing a skirt when he comes, of course. This is Mexico. He wears dark trousers of lightweight wool, a white golf shirt, a jacket, and a flat felt hat. He has brought me a fat gold candle that smells of beeswax. I find a dish for it and set it between us. I pour more wine.

Riley, lifting his glass to his lips, gives me a little wink. At least, I think he does.

"This is wicked of you, Charlotte," the priest says much later, when we've finished a second bottle and I've brought out the brandy. He swirls the brandy in his snifter very expertly. In the candlelight, it has an amber sheen. There's a cold breeze up from the lake, and we move from the veranda into the small dining room, leaving our mess for Nola in the morning. It's pleasant to sit at the clean, clear table, with nothing on it but the gold candle, our glasses, the bottle. I lean back against the fat cushion of my leather chair, and put my bare feet on the table.

"She'll never know," I say, wiggling my toes, meaning Elias's wife, who only comes once a year, at Christmas, when I go away, to the coast, or sometimes to Texas. Neither the priest nor Riley comment. I know I've embarrassed them, though I'm modest enough in my silk trousers, caught at the ankles, harem-style.

I love the sounds of night, the chirping, the rustles in the garden, the slap-slap of the watchman's bare feet along the walks. I love the picture of myself here, in this hidden house the tourists haven't found, the idea of myself without the needs of a common woman.

It's all I can do to keep from weeping.

It is surely the wine.

I tell Luis, "Riley was exclaiming about the beauty of the region." We've discussed the food. The wine. I don't want them to go. I'm too drunk to drive Riley back to Lago, anyway. There are no lights on the road, there's not even a center line.

"They say that this region, and a part of Kenya, are the most perfect climates in the world," Father Luis says. "Temperate all year round. You can see why so many are drawn here."

"But so many leave," I remind him.

"That's something else entirely," he says. "The young people, wanting things the Americans bring with them or leave behind."

"My neighbors Felipa and Oscar came from Guadalajara," Riley says. "Felipa's mother is from a village around here. I have to take my map home so she can place it. I hadn't made the connection until I came. She's always saying she's going to go home, but she's very old, and not very well."

"The young people used to come home every year for fiesta," Father Luis says. "They'd come in their cars, bringing jeans and radios and tapes and contraband TVs. The fiesta lasted all week, when I first came here. The migrants tried to outdo one another. They paid for everything—food, and beer, and fireworks. Then it just dropped off. There'll just be one night this year, but a festive one. Everyone hopes their children will come home, but few do."

"But no one can take away the childhoods," Riley says. Luis and I watch him through the candlelight. There's a bit of the seance to the scene. "The memories are a treasure. A mother, a father—the children—the day-to-day taking care, watching them grow up—"

"If they do," Father Luis says. "If they live that long."

"I'm so sentimental," Riley says, with the hint of a slur.

"This is a healthy village," I say.

"Healthy," Father Luis says, "but not robust. Not economically."

"The tourists—" I begin, but am not sure what I mean to say.

"They bring money," Father Luis says. "They're good for that." He glances at Riley. "No offense."

"I'm not offended," Riley says, but he has grown somber.

"To be out of place, that is the very heart of travel," Father Luis says. He sighs. "To live like a traveler is harder."

"Not belonging?" I say.

"I will forever be the foreign priest," he says. "I have chosen that. I want it. But it is not always easy."

"My wife believed that you traveled to find yourself," Riley says slowly. "We had planned to go to Egypt. What do you think we'd have found there?"

"I remember Mrs. Riley well," Father Luis says. "She had an imposing stature. A kind face. You looked happy. You looked understood."

"I was," Riley says sadly. "For a while, I was."

After Father Bernal is gone, I tell Riley he can sleep in Elias's room. He says he will take a taxi, I'm not to bother, but it's late, and a taxi would have to come from Lago.

"I need to go over early in the morning," I say. "Please, stay." I don't think he's quite as drunk as I am, but neither of us needs to go anywhere.

"We'll have breakfast at the hotel, then," he says.

"I'd like that," I say. It's perfect.

Loza has maneuvered his way between Riley's feet. Riley reaches down to pet him, and Loza rouses enough to throw his paws up on Riley's lap. In one scoop, Riley has pulled him onto his lap. The dog hangs off both sides, but settles with a sigh. Riley rubs his hands down the dog's back. Then he takes an ear. "One ear," he whispers. The other: "Two ears." He taps each paw, counts, and says, "All here, fine dog!" Loza rumbles with pleasure.

I wouldn't mind if he counted me. The company through a night. The warmth. Maybe the pleasure.

I decide I'll leave it entirely up to him.

"Come on, let me show you," I say. Gently, he lets Loza slide to the floor. I take him to Elias's room. It's a handsome room, with a four-poster mahogany bed, a chest with a mirror, even a valet stand. And a bath. "I can't promise the water is hot," I say. "Sometimes yes, sometimes no. But it's wet. There are pajamas in the drawer—" I point to the chest.

"I can get you bottled water—" I reach across him for the decanter on the bureau. How sad, I think, for both of us to be alone.

He rests his arm on the top of the chest. "I'm so tired all of a sudden, I just want to go to sleep," he says. My answer, I guess, if I ever had a question.

"Sometimes the best solace is the closeness of—a friend," I say. My hand, still on the bottle, is close enough that he could touch me if he wanted. There is that lovely sensation that says *flesh*.

"After dinner with a priest?" he says, and smiles.

I take a step, and kiss his cheek. "Good night." I suppose I'm relieved, really. I don't think Tom Riley is sophisticated— or careless—enough for a casual encounter. Besides, I've had a lot to drink, and my sinuses ache.

"Good night," he says, and laughs. Loza has come in behind us and jumped up on the bed. Riley shrugs. "Just like home," he says.

"It is home," I tell him before I go.

I take the fat gold candle to my room and put it on the window. In a small dish, I set the herbs Consolata left me.

"I'll bring him by you on the road," I whisper. It's turned out to be so easy.

I light the herbs. They are sweet, pungent, full of dreams.

A Ride
to Town

TWO AMERICANS IN A JEEP. Two women on the side of the road.

Riley and Charlotte, a little shy with one another.

"Did you sleep?" she asks.

"Sure did," he answers. "Like a log."

He is thinking ahead of Sunday in Lago, along the plaza and the promenade. Maybe, after Mass, a boat ride to an island in the lake. At the craft markets along the shore, he can shop for small gifts. Something for his niece, something for his assistant, Dora. And for Bernadette, of course, Bernadette who once went to Lourdes with her mother.

He likes the mariachi bands, and the musician who sets up by his wife's roasted corn stand with a cowbell and a xylophone.

It's too soon to think about lunch, but he does, wondering if the Patio is open on Sunday.

He likes the señora's cooking.

Consolata.

*   *   *

Divina, free today from the Posada, is dressed in a T-shirt and denim overalls, a gift from Charlotte. Her hair is drawn back in a long ponytail and wrapped with a blue satin ribbon. Out of her pink uniform this morning, she feels smart and pretty. Boys she doesn't know will look at her, and she will pretend she doesn't see them looking. The girls from the city will be in town, wearing outfits with brand names emblazoned on them. She will wait on them, and jump when they call. They like their tables piled with dishes. They take bites from one another's plates. They buy more than they can eat, and linger, drinking beer like water. They leave tips for Divina.

She wants to buy a dozen candles for fiesta, and a comb for her hair.

She is standing with her mother on the side of the road, waiting for the bus. She is thinking now of the dress she hopes her brother Ruben will bring. "Long," she wrote him, "and a bright color. Something a Texas girl would wear to a dance." She didn't dare to ask for shoes.

Her brother replied, "I can't promise anything. Tell Mama I will try."

He sent a money order for fifty dollars, and a new photograph of the children. They are wearing knit caps, tied around their chins.

Charlotte is watching for the women.

She says to Riley, "Look, it's the Arispes, should we give them a ride?" Already she is pulling onto the shoulder of the road.

"Come with us," she calls to them.

"You are so kind," Consolata Arispe says.

"Great," Divina says, in English.

They settle in the back seat. "This is my friend Tom Riley," Charlotte tells them. "Consolata Arispe, and her daughter Divina."

It is a silly, shy moment. The exchange of names, which they already know. The smiles. *Enchanted.*

Charlotte pulls back onto the road. Divina bends forward. Her shoulder almost brushes Riley's.

"Charlotte," she says. "Does your car go fast?"

Charlotte laughs and accelerates, not too much.

Behind the jeep, dust billows. Riley leans back and takes in the vista as they rush along. Hills and houses, the curve of the road ahead.

Consolata pulls her shawl around her shoulders.

Riley takes something from his wallet and turns in the seat.

"Señora Arispe," he says. "I forgot to give you this." He hands her a holy card. "From your village. From the chapel of the Virgin."

Consolata takes the holy card. She tucks it inside her rebozo. "A kind gift, Señor," she says.

"God, what a beautiful day!" Charlotte exclaims. "What a beautiful, beautiful day!" She glances at Riley, who is looking straight ahead.

Divina leans out over the edge of the Jeep, to see better around Charlotte. "Faster!" she says again. She cries out something more, but in the rush of air, no one hears what she says. Her hair whips in the wind.

PART TWO

In Which a Man Finds a Bed in a
Dusty Village,
New Friendships Are Forged,
and Passion Is Ignited

A
Crumbled Cookie

IN THE BAKERY, Yzelda is wrapping hard rolls for Don Pedro in a piece of brown paper. Wearing a big white smock, with a white scarf around her hair, she looks like a doll in too-big clothes. She can't bring herself to meet Don Pedro's eyes. He's a joker, a come-home-again villager with American ways. No local man would tease like he does. Just last week he told her, "Bad luck! All my sons are married, or I'd take your picture and send it to them, prettiest girl in Teca." Teca? Pretty? She blushed six shades of pink. Besides, everybody knows Divina is the most beautiful girl in Jalisco.

She understands a little better when he says, another time, "My wife Cindy is a tiny girl, like you." He did say "is," so this Cindy—she must be living somewhere, no? But there's no sign of her, and he's been here since October, except for two weeks at Christmas when he went away. "Maybe he's looking for a new, village wife," her mother says. "Those migrants, don't a lot of them have two?" She won't

let Eusebio talk about the north. As if she can stop him, once
he makes up his mind.

Yzelda's mother brings in a fresh tray of sugar cookies
and slides them into place on the shelf behind the glass in
front of Yzelda at the counter. "I'll have one of those little
chubbies right now," Don Pedro says when he smells them—
the almost burnt aroma of browned sugar crystals, the hint
of cinnamon. He's wearing a nice American T-shirt with
white piping on the collar. It's snug around his belly, but his
arms look solid. "On second thought, I'll have another," he
says, and stands there chewing it as Divina comes in wearing
her pink uniform.

"Hey Divinita," Yzelda calls. "What's up, girl?"

Just last night, Eusebio told Yzelda, "Tell Divina I'll still
be here for fiesta." He's been helping the schoolmaster with
roof repairs after he comes home from the fields. He doesn't
say what he'll be paid, or what he's planned for the money.
Everybody would make the same guess.

"After that I don't know," Eusebio added, and got a dirty
look from Mama. She sent him outside to water her pots of
chiles on the patio, girl's work, just to shut him up. Yzelda
followed him. "There are other girls," she said, though she
couldn't think who. "There are other places," he muttered in
return.

Divina, bored on the bus, has undone her braids, and her
hair flies out over her shoulders. She has trimmed the sides
to look like a famous model in the magazines, with pieces of
different length. In the back, it still falls to her waist. "Some
bread for supper," she says.

"Oh yeah? Bread with your beans now?" Yzelda says.

"Sure, sometimes I like bread with my *sopa*. Don't you?"
Divina speaks loftily, as if she has a secret—something
stolen, maybe, from the gringo hotel.

Don Pedro takes his packet of rolls and booms out a thank you. "Thank you, too, Señorita," he says when he turns to Divina just behind him.

"Me?"

"Like flowers. Like stars. Pretty girls are sweet for the eyes," he says, and goes out whistling. He's always happy, Don Pedro, even with his Cindy somewhere else.

"I heard he's talked Don Genaro into getting a big dish, like him, for TV at his house," Yzelda says. Lots of villagers have TVs, but they can't get much reliably. Mexican soap operas. Shoot-em-ups. Sometimes *Hawaii Five-O*.

"Maybe Pedro's tired of visitors every night," Divina says.

Yzelda's mother says, "They'll take turns. It's friendlier that way. It's not like Don Pedro is the *patrón*, that way." She holds a cookie out to Divina. "Take it, you're thin as a carrot," she says, looking at Divina's long legs. "Like American girls," she scolds. She goes into the back room to put things away. Later, after supper, she'll come back to put starter out to rise for the baker, who comes at four to make rolls.

Divina nibbles around the edges of the cookie. She sighs.

"Does your mother hear from Ruben?" Yzelda asks. She lifts the skirt of her smock to wipe her forehead. Underneath, she wears a yellow skirt. "Is he going to bring you a new dress?"

"He sent a money order and made no promises about the fiesta."

"He'll come," Yzelda says. "This is home."

"He lives in Texas now. His wife was born there. He's going to be a U.S. citizen one of these days."

"Everybody wants to leave," Yzelda says. "But they all want to come home, too. Back and forth, back and forth. Look at Don Pedro. It took him forty years, but here he is! My mother wasn't born when he left. And he's back. Some of us have to live here, you know, or it won't be a place anymore for them to come back to. It'll just be an idea."

Behind her, in a small tin frame on a shelf, Reymundo's photo sits alongside a candle and a geranium in a pot and a statue of Mary. Yzelda has tied tin rings around the statue's neck, to make Reymundo come home soon.

The bell on the door jangles. It's a gringo.

"Señorita," he says politely to Yzelda. He nods to Divina, too. "Señorita," he says again.

"Señor—" Her voice rises with uncertainty.

"Tom Riley," he says. "Divina, yes?"

Yzelda says proudly, "Divina speaks English, Señor. Go on, Divina, say something."

Riley says, "Now I remember where I've seen you."

In English, Divina says, "Do you have a big car where you live, in the north? Or a little one, like Charlotte?"

"Not too big," he says. "Where I live I can take the bus, and walk a lot." He moves to the counter. He looks back again at Divina, holding her nibbled cookie. He tells Yzelda, "Give me one of those, please."

Yzelda takes his money. Over his shoulder she watches Divina, who hasn't moved.

"At the hotel," he says to Divina.

"The hotel," she says scornfully.

"I've had lunch at your mother's cafe several times."

"That's good."

"And your father?" he says. "What does he do?"

"Here's your bread," Yzelda says quickly. She holds a roll out in each hand.

"My father is dead," Divina says. She puts her cookie in her pocket, and takes the rolls.

Riley squeezes his cookie so violently it crumbles in his hand. "Sorry, sorry," he says, seeing the mess he has made. The cookie is mostly on the floor.

Yzelda comes around with a short straw broom and

sweeps the crumbs into her hand. She puts them in a sack behind the counter and wipes her hands on a damp towel.

Divina looks on.

Riley puts a bill on the counter. "I am sorry," he says again, and backs away.

"I am Maria Divina Arispe." Divina watches the gringo with a cool gaze. "My mother is Consolata Lourdes Arispe. My father saw an owl and died." Before Riley takes another step, she has left the bakery.

Riley looks at Yzelda, who shrugs. He must see that Divina has told him all there is to know.

Dinner on
the Veranda

DOWNSTAIRS ON THE WALK IN FRONT OF THE HOTEL, Riley was
watching for Charlotte's Jeep. She had suggested they meet
early, so that the women could get back to old Filomena and
their chores; they had to get up at dawn. She suggested making dinner herself at the Great House, but he wanted it to be
a treat for her, too. And tonight was special. At the hotel,
they were serving their "All-American" dinner: pot roast with
potatoes and vegetables, pumpkin pie. He thought it would
be fun. Like having them at his house, serving something he
would have cooked himself.

He saw the Jeep and waved. Charlotte was able to park
up the street. He watched them walk the block toward him,
Charlotte between Consolata and Divina. Everyone had
dressed up. Charlotte wore a long gauzy skirt and silk
blouse. Consolata was in a striped shirtwaist dress with a
wide gold belt; her hair was pinned up. Divina was wearing

a long white flounced skirt and a white scoop-necked blouse embroidered with birds all along the yoke. He was glad he'd had a white shirt laundered to wear, himself. He thought they made a handsome party.

He shook hands with everyone. "I'm so glad you could come," he said.

He had extended the invitation through Charlotte on Monday in class. He explained that he didn't want to interrupt Consolata at work, but he knew Charlotte knew how shy he felt. "Do you think they'd want to come to dinner with me?" was the way he'd framed the question. "And you? If it's not too late to ask?"

Charlotte didn't answer right away, which made him even more nervous.

"I thought, who do I have to ask, and who's been nice to me, but you, especially, and Consolata, too, with her hospitality at the cafe. Offering me bites of this and that. Making suggestions. What do you think?"

He didn't think the Mexican women would come without Charlotte, and if they did, he'd feel he was in deep water. How many women had he taken to dinner in his life? His mother, his wife, his sister (and never just the two of them), and, a few times since Eva died, her daughter Bernadette, with one of her roommates. Not much of a social record. It was odd, when he thought about it: that he was most comfortable with women, and yet had known so few. It was so difficult to get past the tongue-tied stage.

Charlotte had said, "If you stop talking, Riley, I'll tell you I think it's fine, and I'll drive us over and we can meet at your hotel."

Then he saw Brenda Flaxman at the pool in the afternoon. She said she and Joe were meeting another couple at a restaurant in a remodeled guest house that was supposed to be quite elegant. She'd heard that the cook had spent a year in training in Houston. Did he want to come? He said he had plans. She looked skeptical.

"I was thinking of asking Renata," she said, "but I leave it up to you." She was grinning, but he didn't see the joke.

"Really," he told her. "I have plans. You're nice to think of me, you'll have to tell me about it tomorrow."

He should have asked more about the restaurant, he thought later. Maybe they could all have gone. Not together. He didn't see Joe Flaxman at his table. But the same place, if it was so special.

He wanted to treat his guests to pot roast, though. He was being optimistic, because the hotel did cater to Americans, and surely somebody would have let them know by now if they didn't do it right.

He took Consolata's elbow gently and led them all up the steps into the hotel. The dining room was actually a large part of the downstairs, just behind the lobby, most of it tucked under the wide winding staircase. Beyond it was the veranda and the gardens and the pool. He'd asked for a table where they could see the gardens.

They walked across the lobby and stood by the headwaiter's station, a kind of lectern on a small table, with a book open to lined pages. There were a few people seated, having drinks. A waiter was just finishing setting a table near the door. He stood back, surveyed the tables, then saw Riley waiting. He took a few steps toward them, halted, and turned back to the kitchen. Another waiter came out, carrying several small vases with flowers. "Oh, hello!" Riley called out. The waiter busied himself with the flowers.

"I suppose it's not his job," Riley said.

Charlotte stepped closer to him. "We're eating here?"

"It's a meal I thought we would enjoy," he said. "Like taking you all home for the evening. Is that all right with everyone?" He looked to Consolata, who said, "As you wish, Señor Riley."

"Only Riley," he said. "Please just call me Riley."

"Cool," Divina said, in English.

The headwaiter crossed briskly toward them.

"Mr. Riley," he said stiffly. "I'm so sorry, you've been waiting?"

"A table for four," Riley said.

"Such a pity. We have no seats for you in the dining room."

"But I spoke to you not an hour ago."

"And I didn't realize. There's a party coming in from another guest house. All the tables—" he swept his arm around, pointing at the almost empty room.

"Back by the French doors," Riley said. "I thought—it's early, we could see the gardens there."

Riley felt Consolata's arm stiffening. Charlotte said, "We can walk up the avenue, Riley."

That would be easiest. He saw that immediately. They would enjoy a walk. There were many restaurants all along the avenue. Charlotte would probably know which was best. But he had thought about this all day. There was something not quite right. He had this feeling, this uneasiness, like a tight fist in his chest. There was something he was supposed to do here.

"We want the pot roast," he said firmly. "There are many tables empty."

"Let me check the reservations," the waiter said. He ran his finger down the page of his book, looking for all the world like an actor cast as a maître d'.

"We'll wait if we must," Riley said, playing his own part. He weakened a little. "Maybe we would be finished before the other party comes."

Charlotte, beside him, shifted position slightly. "I know a nice little place on the beach," she said.

Divina and Consolata were expressionless. They might have been waiting for a bus.

"We'd like to eat right away," Riley said in a loud voice. The couple at a table a few yards away looked over curiously. The woman leaned toward her companion to whisper something.

"Just a moment," the waiter said. He went toward the kitchen and conferred with another waiter. There didn't seem to be any work going on, only consultations.

He came back to Riley's party. "We can seat you and your companions on the veranda," he said, with great politeness. "Since you are interested in the garden."

"Fine," Riley said, relieved.

"It will be a few moments," the waiter said in his same servile voice, which was beginning to bother Riley.

They stood by as two couples came in and were seated promptly. The newcomers had said nothing about a reservation.

"I don't think I like this," Charlotte said. "I don't mean to butt in."

A different waiter waved to them.

"See, they're ready for us," Riley said. They caught up with the waiter and followed him onto the veranda.

A few people sat at bistro tables, having cocktails.

At the end of the veranda, near the kitchen windows, a table had been set up for Riley's party. He pulled out a chair for Consolata, who looked at him, then at the chair. "Sit, please," he said.

"Menus?" the waiter asked. He was quite young, maybe Divina's age. He glanced at her with what seemed to Riley quite like a smirk. "Or shall I tell you what we have?" He held menus in his hand, up at his shoulder, like a fan. His starched white shirt crackled.

"Give us a moment," Charlotte said.

"Would you like to try a dish my mother often made at my home?" Riley asked the Arispe women.

"As you wish," Consolata said.

"A dish of beef and vegetables," Riley explained. "It's called 'pot roast.'"

"Pot roast," Divina repeated. "Pot roast," and she smiled.

"Or we could go somewhere else," Riley said, feeling less bold by the moment.

"Hell, no," Charlotte said. "We're here now, I say let them serve us. It's not a private club." She was agitated. "Surly snobs."

The waiter returned, and Riley ordered. "You could serve us family style," he said. He had seen this done.

"We could do that," the waiter said, that same smirk on his face. He simply could not keep his eyes off of Divina, who appeared to take no notice whatsoever.

"Señor Riley," Consolata said when the waiter was gone. "I have been waiting to hear your adventure. While we are waiting for our dinner—tell us how you passed the night in so humble a village."

The waiter brought a basket of rolls and a pot of butter. He set them on the table with an exaggerated flourish. Then he reached for the carafe of purified water.

"I'll pour," Riley said. As he did so, he said, "I made new friends. I slept like a boy." He thought that the women's blank faces had taken on an attentiveness. He felt welcome at his own party.

Everything took too long. The meal came in pieces, so that the potatoes had cooled before the meat arrived. There wasn't a proper knife to carve the roast, and it wasn't tender enough to pull apart with a fork. The gravy had an unexpected flavor, like licorice, though it wasn't unpleasant, only odd.

He saw that Consolata was looking for something on the table. "What can I get for you?" he asked, but she said everything was good.

"Could we have some tortillas?" Charlotte said.

Of course, Consolata wanted tortillas. He hadn't thought.

Managing to get the tortillas brought to the table wore on his patience. "In a moment," a waiter told him twice. Finally, he put his napkin down beside his place and pushed his chair back. "They ought to send this staff to grade school and start all over," he said. He could just hear his mother saying, Don't make a fuss, Tommy.

"This is delicious," Divina said. "Pot roast." She made the "t"s into happy little explosions.

Riley barely stepped away from the table when a waiter came swooping upon them with the proper basket.

"They're good and hot," Charlotte observed.

Consolata rapidly rolled one around bits of meat and carrot, and ate with zest. "I like it," she said.

Out along the walk and around the pool, two women were taking down paintings that had been displayed on easels for sale. One woman wore a dramatic, brilliant Mexican costume; she had very blond hair and carefully drawn eyebrows. The other woman was dressed in jeans and a T-shirt.

"I wonder how they do," Riley said.

"These painters do all right," Charlotte said. "Though I wouldn't think this would be the best spot."

"Charlotte is painting a picture of me," Divina said. Her mother looked at her with that same indiscernible expression.

"Will we see it?" Riley asked.

"It's a long way from being finished," Charlotte answered. "I'm in over my head, frankly."

"Try these," Consolata said to her daughter quietly. She was pointing to the bowl of overdone peas.

Divina took some in a tortilla and ate a big bite.

"I'm stuffed," Charlotte said, pushing away from the table.

Consolata immediately put her own napkin down. "It was very good, Señor—"

"Riley," Divina said. She pronounced it *Ry-uh-lee.*

"It was only a little good," Riley said, "and only a little American, but I hope you enjoyed it. And I am very glad you came."

"Señor." The headwaiter stood beside Riley.

"Yes?"

"We are needing the table, will there be anything else?"

"We want pie. Pumpkin pie, I believe, tonight?"

"Oh no, Señor, we did not make the pie tonight."

"What is there, then?"

"I would have to ask," the waiter said.

"I couldn't eat a bite," Charlotte said.

"Nor me," said Consolata.

"I'd rather have an ice cream," Divina said. "On the square."

The headwaiter, visibly relieved, laid the check on the table.

"You are kind," Consolata said as they all rose.

No one else was eating on the veranda. The dining room had almost filled with guests of the hotel. They passed through the dining room. Several people were eating pumpkin pie.

On the steps, Riley said, "You had a good idea, Divina."

"It is late," Consolata said.

"Mama—" Divina began, but said no more.

They walked to the Jeep. Riley helped Consolata to her seat.

"Next time—" he said.

"Very kind," Consolata interrupted. She extended her hand.

*   *   *

He walked for fifteen minutes before returning to the hotel.
He didn't know what he ought to do about the service they
had received. Something had been wrong about it. Had he
failed to follow some protocol? Not tipped the right person?
He asked himself how his brother-in-law would have handled
the situation, but Richard would never have brought the three
women to dinner. Margaret would never have allowed it.

The young waiter was leaning against the wall outside
the hotel, smoking a cigarette as Riley approached. He had
taken off his white shirt and loosened his belt. He wore an
undershirt with deep armholes. He pulled himself up and
said good evening.

Riley passed him by, slightly ashamed of himself, slightly
thrilled at his own rudeness. *Now he's pleasant!* he thought.
Now he pays attention! Maybe he was making too much of
the dinner. Maybe they were incompetent with the American menu.

Maybe they hadn't liked his company.

In his room, he rearranged his bedside stand. He pushed
the lamp to the side a little more. He moved his photograph
of Eva so that he could see it from where he would lie. He
took out another photograph, this one of his dogs, and
propped it against the lamp, too.

He sat on the edge of the bed.

"People think they can treat me any way they want," he
complained to Eva. "It was the women, wasn't it? The Mexican women." He was suddenly furious. "I'll see the manager!" he said, but he was so tired, he lay down in his
clothes. He didn't feel the same as he had about the hotel.
He felt out of place. He realized that he didn't enjoy the
company of the other Americans. It wasn't what he had
come to Mexico for. He didn't want to operate on a pedestal
above the locals. He wanted to be among them. He had no

idea what that meant, only that it seemed unachievable and desirable at the same time. As if they knew something he would never know. And all the while, he was probably romanticizing: the wise and pure peasant, like D. H. Lawrence. Hell, it was completely seductive; he understood that book better now. *It's their mystery,* he thought.

"You would have liked her," he whispered. "She is a strong woman, like you. Resourceful and graceful and very kind. You would have been friends."

The
Chorus

THE MANAGER, MR. GUTTMANN, WAS GERMAN, or perhaps Austrian. "It's very awkward, Mr. Riley," he said. They were at the front desk after breakfast. Riley hadn't been able to eat his roll with beans. His coffee tasted bitter.

"Won't you please step into my office?"

"Is that necessary?" Riley asked, but several people nudged close to him, vying for the attention of the clerk. He followed the manager into his office. The manager moved behind his desk, but he neither took a seat nor offered one to Riley.

Riley leaped to the point. "Your waiters were rude to us. And the matter of the pie—"

"We had a baker out ill," the manager said. "We ran short."

"We were squirreled away out of sight. And ignored."

The manager sighed. He brushed a speck of lint from his fine gray jacket. In his careful, clipped English, he said, "Our guests do not expect—really, Mr. Riley, do I need to tell you this? Do not expect to come to dinner and find one of their chambermaids at the next table."

"She was nicely dressed. She is a beautiful girl."

"Nevertheless—"

Riley waited, but the manager didn't seem to think he needed to elaborate.

"She wasn't at work. She was my guest!" Riley said in frustration.

"I have deleted the dinner charge from your bill. You were all guests of the hotel. I hope that is satisfactory."

"You shouldn't have put tomatoes in the roast," Riley said.

The manager shrugged. "You are in Mexico, Señor."

Brenda Flaxman must have been hovering. She was next to Riley the moment he stepped into the lobby. She took his arm. "You look furious," she said. Gleefully, he thought.

"I am furious. I should have done something last night instead of letting these waiters push us around."

"Germans are so stuffy. And waiters are snobs. It's all part of hotel work, don't you think? They hate us, these Mexicans. They hate Indians. They hate themselves. You were a scapegoat for their resentment. I'm sure it's happened before."

"Already you know about it, and you weren't even around."

She squeezed his arm familiarly. "Silly Tom Riley. You are upsetting the order of things. You stir up the natives and then you go back to—is it Ohio? Illinois?—and the wake you leave behind will be our manager's problem. His guilt."

"Whatever are you talking about?" He pulled Brenda along toward the front door.

"I believe he thinks you will leave him with this girl on his hands."

Riley paused in the foyer. He caught a glimpse of a flyer announcing tryouts for *Auntie Mame*.

"Do you understand? You'll take up with his help, and then you'll leave something behind. And he'll have another life weighing on him." She laughed cheerily. "I believe Mr. Guttman is afraid he will have to marry his maid!"

He freed his arm and stared at her. "This is crazy."

"Oh, stop. You don't believe me, do you? You don't know how interested everybody is in you—"

"For heaven's sake, why?"

"Because you are attractive and likable—and available."

"Everyone is very mistaken." Rude as he knew he was, Riley pulled away from Brenda's mockery and hurried onto the street. He heard her call out behind him, "If I'd been here I'd have made a scene for you!"

He walked furiously fast, not along the promenade, but over a few streets, past a few small stores and a block of apartments, past houses and a restaurant and he didn't notice what else. He pumped his arms at his side, forward back forward back, till his heart was racing. He walked down walks and in the street; he dodged a taxi and pickups and a cluster of workmen drilling at an intersection. He made a loop and came out near the market. He went toward the Patio, but paused at the end of the alley. He had to get his breath. Had to think.

He found Consolata at her grill. Already there was a smell of chiles. She smiled and said, "Good morning." He stood on the walk. The grate wasn't pulled all the way up yet; she wasn't open for business.

"I have coffee," she said.

He was perspiring. He patted his forehead with his handkerchief. He couldn't think of any way to apologize to her. She turned to the counter and began chopping onions. He raised his arms to his sides again. "Can't stop," he said. "Exercising—" He gave her a wave.

On the promenade, he slowed down, breathing deeply.

In his room, he showered and changed into a crisp blue short-sleeved cotton shirt and khakis. He packed hurriedly. "Well, Eva," he said as he put her photograph in his luggage. "Margaret was right. I shouldn't have traveled alone."

Outside his room, he stood at the railing of the balcony and looked down on the lobby, the tables now cleared from breakfast. Things were very quiet down there.

At the front desk again, he demanded to see the manager. The clerk, the same pretty girl who had checked him in, rushed away. Guttman came back, moving briskly, his jaw set. "Mr. Riley," he said.

"You tell me this is Mexico, but you're the one who doesn't know where you are. All these people you order around—it's their country. I slept better in a borrowed bed in a village." His voice cracked. "I ate better, too." He caught his breath.

Guttman eyed his luggage. "Will you be paying with traveler's checks or a credit card, Mr. Riley? Miss Jiminez will help you." And he was gone, just like that.

Riley paid, his ears burning. He heard whispering behind him. A trill of laughter. He went to the curb to watch for a taxi.

Les appeared beside him and clapped him on the back. "Sorry to see you go so soon, before we could get over to see the butterflies."

Riley could think of nothing to say. He took a step into the street and looked up toward the square. He spotted a taxi and waved his arm.

Les followed. "If I were you," he said in an annoying, avuncular tone, "I'd try a cruise next time. Lago isn't the place for a single man."

The taxi driver bounded out of the taxi and took his bags and put them in the trunk. Riley got in the back seat. As he pulled the door shut, he saw that there was a cluster of guests on the steps. At least half a dozen. Several waved. Some were laughing, as at the antics of children. One gave him a thumbs-up sign.

"To the airport," he said.

The taxi driver turned. "Forty-five minutes, twenty-five American dollars," he said, in English.

"Fine." Riley slumped into the seat. He hardly noticed as they passed through the town, onto the highway. He kept hearing Guttman—"You are in Mexico."

They were rushing past fields. A bus coming the other direction blew black exhaust.

"Stop, stop!" he said, leaning forward and tapping the driver's shoulder.

The driver braked and pulled to the side, skidding on the broken pavement. He looked into the rearview mirror. "Señor," he said.

"I've changed my mind," Riley said. "There's someplace else I want to go."

The driver glanced at his watch. "Same time, same dollars."

"Slow down a little," Riley said wearily.

The driver shook his head and grinned.

Riley didn't give a damn.

A Bed
in the Village

IN THE CHAPEL IN TECATITLÁN, an old woman was cleaning one of the small side altars. She wiped the plastic flowers and blew softly on a cut gladiolus. She wiped the jars and the statue of the Madonna. She crossed herself and moved forward, dabbing at a spot on the wall. In the front, she genuflected. Then she left. A bird flew in with a squawk and a flutter of wings and perched on a rafter.

Riley sank onto a bench in the back, now alone.

The chapel was cool and peaceful. The bird cooed softly.

He remembered being here with Eva. Her hand in his. After Sunday Mass they drove to a mountain town famous for its cheese. The place had the unexpected delicacy of a Swiss village—a pink church, a plaza with a bandstand of scrolled white iron. There were no other gringos, hadn't been in months, they were told. There was a pageant with many children singing; it went on and on, but they stayed till the end. They spent the night in a small guesthouse. After dark it grew very cold. They snuggled in the bed under a pile of woven blankets. He traced the line of her brow with his finger. He laid his palm over her belly where the long white scar was. She whispered, "I'm sorry about children, Tom." He couldn't speak, his heart ached so. He moved his hand to her breast, but she turned away to sleep. He listened to her breathe. Her gown fell across his bent knee. Ah, how he wished he had told her again that it didn't matter, he wanted only her.

The priest sat down beside him and put his arm across his shoulders. "Can I help?" he said.

"I was happy here once. I thought it might help to be here again. I'd like to stay a few days. There's no hotel. Are there rooms?"

"I have an idea," Father Luis said. "Wait here."

When Riley stepped outside the chapel with Father Luis, he was greeted by Don Pedro, whose gardener took Riley's bags and started off ahead while they talked.

"I've got plenty of room, and you'll call me Pete." The big man shook Riley's hand vigorously. "It'll be fine to have a gringo in my house! But you can't mind a little noise, a little dust. I'm adding on, and doing a little remodeling."

The two of them said goodbye to the priest and went up the hill to Don Pedro's house. There was much commotion on the grounds. A swarm of carpenters were at work on one side, and two men were laying flagstones on the other. They had cut space through a profusion of bushes, each lively with small pink flowers. A girl brushed past carrying a high pile of folded linen.

"You see?" Pete said with apparent pride. "I've put half the village to work bringing the old place up to code." He laughed. "Not that anybody knows what that means!"

He showed Riley a very nice room with a four-poster bed

and a canopy made of cheesecloth. On a table by the bed was a brightly painted earthenware ark, populated with wooden animals. Across the room, on the wall, was a bright tin mask with a long beard of string, and near where they stood, a collection of small wooden figures: a bird, a man with a strange headdress, and what seemed to be a leg in a boot. "Whatever?" Riley wondered aloud.

"Slingshots. I have a fondness for them. When I was a little boy, it was my job to sit in the field just planted, and keep the birds and rodents away. I've collected them for years. I buy them from children along the road."

"I am delighted, Pete. You do me honor."

"You know what we say," Pete said. "My house is your house."

"Of course I will pay you. And I will try not to be in the way."

"Oh, no. I don't want your dollars. I have a pension from the electricians' union in Stockton, California! What I want is company. Father Bernal didn't tell you I'm a talker, did he? He made you think I was doing you a favor." He was a hearty man.

The gardener had put the bags on the floor by the bed.

"I'll talk to my maid," Pete said. "We'll have an early lunch."

"I couldn't."

"This afternoon I'm going to visit the little *rancho* where I grew up." Pete struck a pose and sang, "Gonna take—a sentimental journey—You'll come too. You'll see how the real folks live. My brother is still there. He raises chickens and corn. We'll take a ride in the hills."

Riley fell under Pete's spell. He couldn't resist his enthusiasm. "Whatever you say, Pete," he said. "I haven't got anything else to do. Except I've got to call my sister. Can you tell me how to get to the long-distance phone office?"

"I wish you could call from here. I've been waiting a month for my phone. Come on, we'll go down there now."

Riley followed him into the kitchen. "Lupita, this is Señor Riley," Pete said. "We want our lunch in an hour or so. Señor Riley's going to be staying with us awhile."

"A short while," Riley said.

Lupita was short and plump, with beautiful golden skin. She giggled and turned her head.

It took half an hour or more for Riley to get through to his sister. She was beside herself. "You did what? A village? What are you going to do in a village?"

"I'm staying with a retired American," he said. "I'm going to stay for fiesta."

"Give me his number."

"He doesn't have a phone yet. In an emergency, you can call this office. Someone has to come get me."

"Don't drink the water, Tom," she said.

"I won't even brush my teeth, Margie."

At lunch, Pete asked Riley if he had boots. When Riley said he did not, Pete sent Lupita to his bedroom to fetch several pair. "Here, try these. You'll want boots, riding through the brush. Even if we have to stuff the toes."

"I didn't realize," Riley said. "I've never been on a horse."

Pete laughed. "Hey, that's okay. We'll ride burros. They're much closer to the ground."

Gossips

EVERY FEW DAYS the old women gather in front of the chapel courtyard, near the street. The schoolchildren have bought Tiburcia's coconut drinks and run off to play. The sun has slipped down so that a long shadow falls across the women's spot. One of them shows up, carrying a straightbacked chair. Usually it is the candy maker's mother, Imelda, from up the street. Soon there's another to sit beside her, her rosary wound in her fingers. That's Elpidia, the carpenter's wife, who sells Chiclets from her bedroom window. Tiburcia puts her jugs and cups in a child's wagon and pulls it behind them, then sits down, waving a piece of cardboard like a fan. Three in a row, like ducks at a fair, they have come to talk.

Leave it to the men on the square to talk about the weather, the crops, the animals. Leave politics to them. The women know what matters. Sometimes they speak of the past, for they are the village historians. They talk as if long-ago events happened just the other day. They tell about soldiers who came into the village without warning, scooping up girls, shooting men and boys. They tell about the days when the statue of the Franciscan in the village fountain spouted water over the head of the kneeling Indian, and of the day the water stopped. They speak of sons gone north, gone to cities, gone to God. They repeat what they have been told of the *hacendado's* family—the hanging chandeliers and long polished tables, the couples in beautiful clothes dancing on gleaming floors. They remember the priest who loved fat Immaculata and kept her children on a *rancho* in the hills.

And then, sighing, they remember where they are.

Imelda brings them to Pedro. "I remember that boy in my yard, slapping my laundry hanging on the line. He came to chase my turkey, and I took him home by the ear."

Their comments roll one to the other. "Now he struts around like the turkey cock himself."

"I saw him kiss you, Doña Imelda, here on the street after Sunday Mass."

Imelda touches her cheek. "Only here," she says, and bites her smile. "Because I am his godmother, all that's left of his old family. He's a good boy who came to see his mother every year until she died."

"My grandson saw Pedro and the gringo on burros in the hills Wednesday, taking the country air, you suppose." Elpidia caws with pleasure. "Laughing like jackasses."

"Did you see the gringo hobbling to the pool hall on Thursday? They'll have to have given him cushions while they watched their movies after dark."

"Sexy American movies," one says disapprovingly.

"You've seen them?" teases another.

Elpidia grasps her knee through the layers of black skirt. "Ay," she moans. "Soon you'll have to carry me around on my chair."

"Don't say," another teases. "Didn't I see you on the plaza Saturday night, swinging on the arm of Don Genaro?"

"Not me!"

"And Pedro and the gringo, singing at the top of their lungs."

"They tipped the band ten American dollars, I heard."

"They should have paid the rest of us to listen!"

And they cackle.

Elpidia says, "Last night I couldn't sleep. I rose to breathe at the window, and below, on the street, I saw Genaro lurking like a dog in the dark."

"Waiting for the all clear from Consolata Arispe," says another.

"Waiting for the gringo to go back to Don Pedro's house."

"My granddaughter stopped by with limes to sell, and what do you think she saw but the gringo filling corn husks with *masa.* 'Have I got enough yet? Do I fold it like this?' he asks."

"A gringo cooks!"

"At the cooking school of Consolata Arispe."

"I've heard him going home at night, whistling Yankee tunes."

"But I see Don Genaro and the gringo on the plaza, drinking beer together."

"Working on fiesta plans, I hear."

"Refugio is building a Catherine wheel. I hear Pedro is paying for all the fireworks."

"Poor Refugio."

"Aaah," they sigh.

They all know why Refugio is to be pitied, but Imelda cannot help saying, "They say his youngest daughter crawled through a window in the night and ran off with young Giberto to his parents' house. Antonio Alvarez and Jesus Benitez were lying drunk in the street and thought they dreamed it."

"Juanita saw them embracing at the gate."

"That decides a wedding." They look solemn at the mention of marriage. "Though no one knows, of course, if they slept that night, or sat outside to count the stars."

"Only that they were together. She won't be skinny long."

"Ay, it's Doña Filomena." Filomena walks slowly toward them, leaning on the arm of Divina.

"I'll come back after I've gone for eggs, Tía," the girl says.

"Forget that," the others say. "We're not so old, we'll help her home."

Divina almost skips away. Filomena sinks onto the stool someone has brought for her. She spits on the dirt and rubs it with her foot.

"You've got a new suitor, so I hear," they tease. "Does he bring you tuberoses for your garden? Does he bring you thread for your doilies?"

"He is a kind man," Filomena says lightly.

"He seemed a sober man," another observes.

"Until the night on the plaza," says another.

"I'd gone to bed and the last thing I saw through my window was the gringo on the street."

"Visiting," one says so that she almost sings it.

"Still he's up early, prancing on the road with his arms cocked like levers."

Filomena says, "He brings us a kilo of sugar. He brings cold drinks and a book for the girl. He carries photographs of his dogs. He asks me about the old days. Every day he wears a clean shirt. Isn't this a good man?"

"You've been a widow all too long," they tease.

"Sixty years," Filomena says. "Sixty happy manless years."

"You were a capable farmer, Filomena," the next oldest woman, Imelda, says. She was a child when Filomena's brawling husband met his match in a drunken fight. "My mother always said yours were the finest pumpkins."

"And everyone knows you were shrewd with a peso," says another.

Filomena nods her head. Her eyes flutter and close.

"He's charmed her," they agree.

"He's charmed the witch."

"Watch what you say. Who knows this?"

"Don't you see her in the hills searching for her weeds? Don't you see her patch of herbs behind her house? The candles burning in her room at night?"

"You've never burned candles?"

"I have burned herbs," admits Imelda. "For the nightmares of my grandchildren that lingered in the house."

Filomena's eyes pop open. "Consolata has been like a daughter to me. She's known hard years."

"Yes, but she's had a home. In your house."

"Her house now," Filomena amends. "What need do I have of anything but a bed?" She sighs. "I dreamed again last night of a soldier."

"Ay, Filomena!" the others say. They can see it was not a bad dream.

"And beside me, the girl dreamed of white houses."

"You know this?"

"I felt the light on my face from the sun on the walls. I felt the shimmer of curtains at the windows."

"She ought to marry." This most sternly spoken.

"Eusebio is losing patience," in the same tone.

"She will settle for nothing less than her dream," Filomena says. She pulls her shawl tighter.

"We all settle for less," the women say. "We all take what we can get, to stay alive."

Tiburcia yawns and gets up to pull away her wagonload of sticky jars. Then the others are up, too, storing what was said and what was unsaid: A gringo courts a witch. A foolish girl aims too high. A migrant brings back his northern ways. An old, old woman slips toward heaven day by day.

Fresh
Cheese

"THIS IS PRETTY SNAZZY," I said. I was in the back seat of Pete's Buick sedan. It was ten years old, in perfect condition. He had reupholstered the seats in crushed velvet.

"I was going to rent a car," Riley said, "but he wouldn't have it any other way. He said, 'You want Doña Filomena to be comfortable.' I couldn't argue with that."

Tía Filomena was sleeping in the back between Consolata and me. In the front, Divina sat forward, taking everything in eagerly. We were on the south side of the lake, headed to Mary of Tears.

I pointed ahead. "Just past that turnoff, there's an arroyo with basins that fill from a spring. After the rains the trickle is a waterfall for a little while. I was there a few years ago. I've meant to go again. It's a beautiful spot. If it were less remote, you can be sure there'd be a hotel there. As it is, I don't think tourists ever hear of it.

"And they say there's a geyser somewhere farther in the

hills," I added. "With water hot enough to boil an egg."

Divina looked around at me impishly. "You would come out very clean."

We laughed, even Consolata.

We stopped in town before going to the village. Riley took us for lunch to the hotel where he had rented the room he never used, the night he stayed in Mary of Tears. The attached restaurant had tables out on the sidewalk and in a small courtyard to the side. Some of them had colorful umbrellas. Riley told the waiter we would need one of the larger ones, with plenty of shade. "And a cushion for the señora," he said. Tía Filomena's scarf was wound low on her forehead. Her eyes were wide open. She looked like a black bird. I saw her eyeing someone's plate of roast chicken.

The waiter showed us a table in the back, but Riley told him it wouldn't do. "We want to sit in the front where we can watch the square and the pedestrians." The waiter opened his mouth to offer some protest—you could tell by the pained expression—but Riley spotted the very table he wanted and held his hand up to stop the words. "Right over there," he said with authority. We stepped past a table of men in suits and tinted aviator glasses. Riley told the waiter, "Bring us lemonade and rolls and tell us what the cook says is best today." He pressed some coins into the waiter's hand and, over his shoulder, winked at me.

"At your orders," the waiter said, suddenly efficient. Off he hurried, and returned with all we needed, even a cushion.

Consolata helped Filomena into a chair beside her, and the old woman's head drooped toward her shoulder. We ordered chicken and rice and squash. The waiter said there was a special fresh cheese today, from Mazamitla. Riley told him we'd want a lot of that with tortillas right away.

One of the suited men snapped his fingers and made the

rude kissing sound common to call waiters. He held an empty beer bottle up by the neck. The waiter scurried over.

The air was fresh, with the slightest breeze, and the sunlight warm and yellow. People strolled across the plaza, and young mothers sat on the benches watching their small children. The cheese was crumbly and salty and white and tasty, and we remarked on it. Filomena broke off small chunks with her fingers and put them in her mouth, then worked them with much gnawing and smacking. So absorbed, she paid no attention to the rest of us.

"Why isn't all cheese like this?" I wondered. I seldom was able to get good cheese or butter, even in Lago.

The waiter, passing by, heard me. "In the mountain town the cows eat the greenest grass and sun themselves by sweet water," he said.

I looked to see if Riley had understood. Indeed, he said to the waiter, "I'd like some to take with me. Can I get it here?"

The waiter, who knew where his bread would be buttered, bent close and confided, "There are hills of it in the market, for it came just this morning. It would be much cheaper there, Señor."

We took our time. Filomena ate some of the rice, and sucked on a chicken bone from Consolata's plate. The businessmen left, eyeing Divina one last time.

"Look at her pretty dress! Look at her hair!" Divina said, pointing to a young woman who walked by. Her hair was cut chin length, so that it swung as she walked. "She is a rich girl," Consolata said, but the material of the dress was not all that fine.

The table was cluttered with the remains of our lunch. "Does the town look much changed?" Riley asked Consolata.

"I was a child. I thought it was a great city. I remember the streets were much wider," she said, and laughed. "I remember coming to market. We brought produce from our field. On a Saturday, the square would be filled with people in from the villages and the countryside. The women wore long skirts and wrapped their heads with shawls. The children who worked were dressed like little adults. The ones who didn't work wore their white communion clothes. When we'd sold our produce, Papa bought us tacos from a street vendor, little scraps of barbecued goat, maybe from the head, the cheapest meat. It was delicious. We went home in the dark. You'd see country people on the road walking miles home. On the bus, the men would sing, if they weren't too drunk. I thought everyone who lived in a town like this was rich. But I don't remember thinking I wanted to live here. I don't remember thinking I wanted to leave the village. I knew these things would be decided in some way I didn't understand. There was no thought of planning the future. You waited for it." She seemed, by now, to be talking to her daughter, who caught her eye, then looked away.

Riley fiddled with a spoon on the table. "As I listen to you, Consolata, I find myself thinking, my life was like that, too. The way I followed along as it revealed itself to me. In all ways you could see, it was unlike yours—a city life, a privileged life, I know—but it was the life given to me and I lived it, as you did yours. Is anyone's life different?"

I laughed, but it was a harsh sound. "I fought mine every step of the way. The first thing I remember thinking was, Let me out of here."

Divina was watching us, her head cocked slightly. I thought she didn't understand what we were talking about. She was a new generation. She was a little impatient; she was young. I saw Riley glance at her; he saw it, too.

"Let me find the cheese, and we'll go to the village," he said.

Filomena had dropped off to sleep. Consolata gently brushed away bits of rice from her chin. "Tía has heard it all," she said. "She's seen it all."

"Would you want to wait while I run to the market?" Riley asked. "So we don't disturb your aunt."

"She is the great-aunt of my mother-in-law," Consolata said. "She has been like a mother to me. I would never leave her."

I said, "I'll stay, too." I was drowsy and content.

"Divina?" Riley said.

She looked to her mother, then said, "I want to walk. The day is so beautiful. And it's so boring sitting here."

"Shh," from Consolata.

"Good," Riley said. "You can choose fruit for us for later."

They went off and we sat like idle ladies at our table under the umbrella, while the waiter cleared our dishes. He brought us a fresh jug of purified water, and clean glasses. Consolata asked for a slice of lime. I was glad to see her relaxing, enjoying the service. That morning, she had gone before dawn into Lago to cook for the cafe, then left it in the care of Yzelda and her cousin for the day.

In twenty minutes or so, Riley returned carrying fat rounds of dripping cheese in a basket, and Divina carried mangoes and limes in another. Riley said, "It's beautiful stuff. I got some for all of us, Pete too. And I thought I'd take some to the people who put me up in the village." He patted a brown paper packet lying on top of the cheese. "I bought hard candies for the children."

Tía Filomena was awake. She was eyeing the packet. "Would you like a candy, Tía?" he asked affectionately. He unwrapped the packet and chose a bright red piece and handed it to her. She slipped it into her mouth behind the screen of her hand. Consolata helped her up from the chair.

"Wait a moment," Riley said, pulling his camera off his

shoulder. He stepped back to get us all in. Filomena, shorter by a foot than Consolata, strained to be seen. Her chin was up; we could see the bulge of the candy in her cheek. "Got it," Riley said, and Filomena sat back down.

"Now you, Riley," I said, and took the camera. Consolata and Divina made a space between them, and Riley stepped in. I waved a hand. "Stand a little closer." They moved in tighter. Behind Riley's back, mother and daughter reached to hold hands. "Say cheese," I said in English. Riley and Divina did, and everybody laughed.

Riley drove into the village so slowly I could have counted the stones. He told us about falling from his seat on the bus. "The pig thought it was funny," he joked. So did we.

There was a vendor outside the church. He greeted Riley like an old friend. "Hey, Señor!" he cried, stretching out his hand. He picked up one of his ropes and dangled it. "You come back for the penance, eh?" Across the way from the church a woman and her young daughter sat on a woolen blanket on which they had spread their wares: strips of chitterlings, wads of candied fruit, some small woven bags, not as big as a wallet.

Filomena was snoring in the back seat. Consolata said she would stay with her while we went inside.

"Of course you won't," I said. "This is your church. I'll stay." We folded Consolata's shawl and tucked it under Filomena's head. Lying down, she was no bigger than a child. Her nut-brown face was criss-crossed with deep lines. She had no eyebrows, but did have a faint mustache of wispy white hair.

Consolata thanked me and went inside. I leaned back in the front seat and thought nothing. Somewhere close by someone was pounding wood. Over by the bar, two men were chipping at the wall of the building and whistling. As I sat there, other sounds came up like bubbles on water. Small children playing. Women chatting and laughing. *Ranchero* music from the bar.

Divina and Riley came out of the church. I went over and stood with them in the shade by the door. Divina whispered, "Mama is crying." I squeezed her hand.

The woman and child were gone with their wares. A boy went by, prodding two black pigs ahead of him with a long stick. Consolata came out from the church dabbing at her eyes. She said, "If we have time, I'd like to walk around."

"We have whatever time you want," Riley said. "We have come for you."

"Accompany me, Divina," Consolata said. "I'll show you where I lived as a girl." She took a deep breath. "It was on the edge of the village—" She pointed. "Over there."

"Tía is sleeping soundly," I said. "I'll keep looking after her."

"I'll go to the house of Cayetano," Riley said. "I hope someone is home."

I went back to the car and took a dreamless nap. I was grateful for the bliss of an empty mind.

Consolata and Divina returned with an old woman and two little girls. "Oh, Charlotte," she said. "I found my mother's sister and her grandbabies. My cousin is in the hills at his corn plot." The old woman was crying, tears rolling down her face, though she was smiling and bobbing her head, as if to confirm that this was happening. "Everyone has been gone for years," Consolata said. "How lucky to find Tía Guadalupe!" She clasped the old woman's hand. The children ran around us in a circle. As they passed Divina, they slapped at her ruffled skirt and she took a few steps and swung her arms, pretending to chase them.

I said, "Riley's camera is in the car. I'm sure he'll want a picture."

The women and girls crowded together on the church steps. I took several shots. Then they talked, too rapidly for me to follow, while we waited for Riley. One of the girls came over and took my hand. She must have been about four years old. She pressed her face against my hip. I bent down. "What's your name?" I asked, but after all her flirting, she was too shy now to speak.

When Riley reappeared he had to be introduced, and there was a lot of handshaking and exclamations. He had delivered his presents to a daughter of the family, who was watching the babies, he said.

I told Riley I had taken a photograph.

"One more," he said, "just to be sure." He moved around to get the light just right.

"Let's have our mangoes," he suggested. Divina took the fruit from the car, and he produced his pocketknife and sliced them carefully on the hood of the car. Then he sliced limes and squeezed the juice over the ripe orange flesh of the mangoes. He gave the first pieces to the children, who carried them away to sit in the dirt in the shade of the church wall.

He took a slice over to the old vendor by his ice cream cart.

"What is it? Where am I?" Out a car window, Tía Filomena leaned so far she looked about to topple. Consolata ran to help her out.

Sticky trails of juice ran off the car into the dust, drop by drop. Consolata coaxed Filomena over to the others and gave her a slice of mango. Filomena smacked it with her gums.

Guadalupe and the children hugged Consolata and Divina hard and left. They all seemed satisfied by the little while they had spent together. When we got ready to leave, I would tell Riley about the cousin, and see if it was possible to drive to his plot. I was sure Consolata would never mention him.

"More pictures," Riley said. "I have six left."

Divina stood on the steps, turned slightly, looking over her shoulder. Her shapely calves showed from under the flounce of her skirt. She was wearing sandals, and her feet were dusty from the walk through the village.

Consolata stared straight into the camera, her arm resting on the stone rail.

Riley took a photograph of me with Consolata and Divina.

He caught Filomena sitting on a step, her knees almost to her chin. She didn't notice that the camera was pointed at her, although Riley knelt to take the shot.

"Now the three of you," Riley said. "A good one I can give you in a frame."

Filomena is between Consolata and Divina. Juice clings to the corners of her mouth. She isn't sleepy now. She has a lively, attentive look. Her eyes sparkle. Divina says something I can't catch. The women laugh. Tía Filomena's mouth opens wide. I look at Riley, ducked a little for the shot. He takes the picture, covers the lens, and hangs the camera on his shoulder. The women are still standing together, as if frozen by the camera in that single moment.

With his handkerchief, Riley wipes the juice from the hood of the car and then leans against it—unhurried, happy, a perfect host.

A
Chided Lover

I walked home from Pete's through the village, enjoying the smells of food, the chatter of children, the music from radios. As I turned the corner and started up the long street to the Great House, I saw Elias's Cadillac. I dug in my bag for a brush to smooth my hair, tucked in my blouse, and went inside.

He was on the veranda, looking at a magazine. There was champagne in an ice bucket and two glasses, ready for my return. I bent to kiss the top of his head and saw that the magazine was something architectural. I caught a glimpse of glass and steel, a double-page spread. I put my hand on his shoulder and he reached up to caress it.

"They told me you had gone off in a big gringo car," he said. "With a man from Chicago."

"And did they tell you we were accompanied by two women?"

"Only after they let me think about it."

"You, my landlord."

"No one thinks otherwise."

I laughed. "No one would say to you. Or me."

I sat down. Elias opened and poured the wine. "I'm on my way to Colima. I couldn't just drive by."

"I'm glad," I said, though I was tired. Elias was, as always, dressed impeccably in expensive clothes. Those men today at lunch—they would love to be Elias Santos, I thought. A man who has everything: a factory, investments in the U.S., a wife from an old and important family. And a mistress. Mistresses, probably. I hoped not.

He was my friend, someone I had been able to talk to from the beginning. I think he liked it that with me there was nothing to prove. No one was watching. And I paid my rent.

We drank our wine slowly as it grew dark.

He said, "It's so peaceful. I should spend more time here."

"You'd be bored."

"You're not?"

"Boredom is soothing. It's a kind of meditation."

He touched my cheek. "Why the long face, dearest?" He was a great fan of old American movies. I suspect he perfected a lot of his English, watching them.

"I'm exhausted," I said. "I came too close to life today. Stood too close to real emotion." I told him about Consolata, and about Riley's night in the village.

"He's lucky someone didn't rob him. Or worse."

"You're too cynical. It comes from living in the city."

"It comes from experience."

"I didn't go in the church. I missed my chance to see a weeping Madonna."

He poured more wine.

"There's more to the story," I said. I felt like talking after all. "Consolata came to me recently." I told him about her visit that night.

He laughed. "It will never happen. He will go back to Chicago with his photographs and put them away and forget all about these village women."

"Probably," I said, only to be agreeable.

Someone from the children's residence was walking in the gardens. I thought I heard a woman crying. Elias heard, too. He shook his head, as if to say: *Everywhere, there is sorrow.*

Instead, he said, "I am thinking I will build you a small house."

"Are you evicting me?"

"Of course not. It will take a long while. But the Great House is, technically at least, my wife's property too. My children's. You should have something of your own."

"Who knows how long I'll stay? My mother wants me to come home to Texas. I wouldn't have to worry about money."

"You know you wouldn't have to worry about money here, either. If you would let me help you. And if you don't want the house, I'll rent it. In the morning we'll walk over to the lot. It's a piece of Don Ramon's orchard. You can see the lake from the property."

"It will be an excuse for you to come more often," I said.

"Another reason to build it." He smiled.

I took more wine. "Elias, do you think I am a cold woman?"

"I think you have buried your heart too deep."

"I feel so little. Everything is a curiosity."

"Curiosity is surely a sign of life."

"I watched Riley today. The way he followed Consolata's motions. Coaxed her to speak. I thought: Here's a man who thought he had one story—that he was loved, past tense.

Now he feels something for Consolata Arispe. She isn't even pretty."

"You'd like him for yourself?"

"Oh, no, he's much too good a man for me. The kind who remembers birthdays and says his prayers. What I'd like is to understand Consolata. Her tough serenity. I feel there's something to be learned from her. I think that's what attracts Riley."

"Village life will grow tiresome. He's not a writer, too, is he? Not someone with a need to hole up? I predict he'll be gone soon. That will be that."

"But he feels something now. Something that has already made him bolder."

Elias poured the last of the wine. I couldn't remember drinking the last glass.

He said, "I don't know what woman is your Consolata. But I am sure I would not find her attractive."

"No. Because she would never need you."

"I was thinking of her looks. Short. Dark. Older than her years. The terrible clothes these women wear."

"Is that what you like about me? My looks?"

"It's one of the things."

"If there's more wine," I said, "I would drink it. I'd like to be drunk."

"What a waste, when you're not alone." He turned my chair and knelt in front of me. He undid my hair. I leaned back and shook it free. He unbuttoned my shirt and slipped his hands inside. I felt my breasts swell to press against his palms. He pulled up my skirt and kissed my thighs.

"So you see—I'm not cold, am I?" I whispered. I could feel my pulse in my inner thigh, where his lips touched. He spoke without raising his head, his voice muffled. "Would a good man do this?"

I lifted his chin and put my finger on his lips. I slid from the chair to the tiles, onto my knees. I was cold inside, but my flesh was warm. I could see us there, a picture of amorous drama; I wondered what movie we were out of.

"A good man—a shy man—can feel desire," I said. "If I wrote his story, I would uncover a passion that stirred the reader—" That stirred me, I thought.

Elias laughed and pulled back. His hands were on my shoulders. "If this foolish notion—this plan—works out. If love triumphs over all its international barriers. If you write your story, dear, dear Charlotte. Then I will buy a bell for the padre's chapel. I will ring it myself for God to hear."

"It's the villagers' chapel. That would be a good gift."

"And when I hear it ring, I'll say, 'God is love.'" He laughed again, with enjoyment.

"You are a blasphemer," I said.

"An adulterer."

"My friend," I said. I moved his hands to my waist.

"Your lover."

He stood and pulled me to my feet.

On his bed, he whispered, "I do love you, Charlotte." He was unabashedly romantic. Undoubtedly, he had professed his love to many women. Still, it was nice.

I couldn't give him a generous reply. "I don't think I've ever loved—"

"Shh. Pretend, foolish girl. Love can be won by loving. You must court it. Say it. Come on, say it."

"Love." I managed the single word.

Soon after, he spoke into my ear. "Again, Charlotte. Say it now. In this moment, everything is true. Say 'love.'"

He was most persuasive. And he would be gone tomorrow.

Don Genaro stands in the shadows across from Consolata Arispe's house, smoking a cigarette. He is leaning against the wall in front of a neighbor's house.

There is light in Consolata's house, and the lamp is lit in her hut. He throws the butt of his cigarette to the ground and steps on it.

The priest appears beside him.

Genaro says, "The gringo isn't there tonight."

"I saw him at the phones a little while ago," the priest says.

"Maybe they are tired from their day. A trip in Pedro's car."

"It isn't late. You would find Consolata awake, don't you think?"

"What would I say? I am full of angry questions," Genaro says.

"Tom Riley is a kind man."

"What does he want?"

"The company of friends."

"Who is Consolata to him!"

"She is the same as you know—a good woman."

"I've been her friend for twenty years."

"You've been more than that, Don Genaro."

"When that brute Elizondo beat her, I ran him out of town, never to be seen again."

"I've heard this," the priest says.

"When she painted her house, I gave her the paint at less than cost."

"And did you help with the labor?"

Genaro stiffens. "In the day, I'm busy with my store."

"And when she was ill two years ago, with a flu we thought would kill her, did you take your turn by her bed?"

"That is for the women to do."

The priest puts his hand on Genaro's shoulder. "The gringo will be gone soon."

"I am waiting."

"But Consolata will not be the same."

"She will be Consolata as always."

"The gringo is a good man. You know this."

"He's amiable. He buys his rounds."

"He has shown her his friendship in the light of day, for everyone to see. He has taken her and her daughter—even the old aunt—to see sights. He has taken them to restaurants."

"He has money, a gringo."

"It isn't a matter of money, Genaro. I think you know this. It is a matter of pride. Hers, now."

In the long silence, Genaro lights another cigarette. Consolata comes out of her hut and crosses to the house and enters.

"You could speak to her," the priest says. "You could tell her how you feel."

"I have loved her a long time."

"An ill-kept secret, my friend—yet, undeclared, not really true."

"My son would not understand."

"Your son lives in Guadalajara. Your wife has been dead ten years. This is your concern."

"It has always served, the old way."

"And now?"

"He'll leave," Genaro says stubbornly. "He'll leave and we will see, Consolata and I, what is there."

At the Arispe house, the young man Eusebio appears from the street and knocks. Divina opens the door. She turns back, calls something, then steps outside. She and Eusebio talk for a few moments. Eusebio's voice rises: "Everyone sees!"

Divina leans to kiss him lightly. She says something more, and then goes back inside.

"Look what the gringo's done," Genaro says.

"What he's done doesn't matter, my friend," the priest

says. "All that matters is what you will do. Start by thinking: What does this woman mean to you?"

Genaro takes a long drag and blows it out, away from the priest. "We'll use the baker's pickup to go for the Madonna for the fiesta. I have received my order of a thousand candles. We'll be ready, Father."

"I will bless the candles Sunday at Mass," the priest says. "I will pray for you tonight. I will pray for lovers everywhere."

A
Wake

IN THE NIGHT, DIVINA FEELS TÍA FILOMENA SHIFT BESIDE HER. She hears her say, "Let them talk." She sits up to look at the old woman. She feels her wrist, cool to the touch, and her throat, which throbs with her dream. She goes back to sleep.

"*Mami, Mami!*" she cries out softly when she wakes at dawn.

Filomena is gone, in the soft, inabrupt rightness of death at a very old age.

Consolata hurries to the house of the old carpenter, whose only work these days is window frames and the occasional coffin. Though it is barely light, he is already in his shed, seated on a stool, drinking hot chocolate. He has had the pieces ready for tiny Filomena for a long time. He will put them together as soon as he wakes his grandson. He clasps Consolata's hand. "She was fiery and smart and good. God will have a place for her." He makes the sign of the cross.

On the way home, Consolata calls on Elpidia, who wraps her rebozo around her shoulders and accompanies her back to her house. Divina has made coffee and warmed tortillas. There is a little of the cheese from the mountain town. The three women eat. While Consolata and Elpidia heat water to wash the body, Divina takes all the doilies down from the wall and lays them on the corner of the bed near Tía's feet. Then she dresses in her pink uniform, goes to tell the priest that Tía is dead, and goes to work.

There is no bell to ring, but by evening, all the village knows. Chairs line the street in front of the little house, and the walkway to the door. Dozens of villagers at a time are there to pay their respects to the oldest villager, Doña Filomena. On the patio, the women have prepared a hominy stew with pork. There is tequila, sent over by Don Genaro. On the table, Filomena lies in the casket, which is lined with a layer of padded satin. She is dressed, as always, in a black dress and a scarf wound low on her forehead. She holds a crucifix. All over her are the doilies, a blanket of stitches, and at her feet, a heap of tuberoses, whose fragrance fills the room.

Consolata sits in a chair by the table. At the foot of the casket is a plate for alms, spilling over with coins. The rapid mutter of the rosary rises and falls in the room. Women bring cups of tea with cinnamon from the patio for other women.

All night they come and go. Always, someone is speaking the rosary in a rapid monotone, like a chant.

Just before dawn men gather to act as pallbearers. The lid of the casket is nailed shut. The men carry the casket to the chapel for the Mass of the Dead. The chapel is overflowing with mourners. Every villager has known Filomena since childhood.

The baker backs his pickup up to the church doors and the pallbearers lift the coffin into the bed. Consolata and Elpidia climb into the cab with the baker. Dozens of villagers follow, walking through the village, across the highway, and up to the cemetery on the slope of a hill from which the lake is visible. Two goats are munching on grass on overgrown headstones. They pay no attention to the men and women who gather to watch the body of Filomena lowered into her grave.

Consolata throws a handful of dirt on the casket. Divina, beside her, crosses herself. Eusebio presses his way to her side. The priest mumbles a prayer.

Riley, on the edge of the group, watches Consolata. *She has such dignity,* he thinks. She is strong and wise, an altogether admirable woman.

He sees Eusebio take Divina's hand.

So who needs Consolata now? The old aunt is gone and Consolata is free.

Charlotte will know, he thinks, though he hasn't formed a question.

He hurries away as the crowd disperses.

The
Pool

A FEW DAYS AFTER FILOMENA'S FUNERAL, two days before the
fiesta, on an afternoon when I was scheduled to work with
Divina, I saw Riley on the street at noon. There had been a
January chill in the morning air, but it was balmy now, a perfect winter day. The sky was like a painting, a flawless, silky
blue, and I longed to be outside. I stopped to chat with him.
He had been working on a float for the fiesta.

"What would you think of going to the pool?" I asked.
"The basins I told you about. It's not a very long drive."

We decided to go over to Lago to have lunch at the Patio,
and there I asked Consolata if she minded Divina going with
us. "I'd sketch there," I said. "We would only be a couple
hours."

She suggested we go to the bakery and see if Yzelda
could go. "You'll have to coax her mother," she said, "but tell
her I sent you."

Yzelda was wild to go. "Please, oh please," she begged

her mother, who pursed her lips and put a fist to her hip and hemmed and hawed and said oh what was the world coming to, but finally relented and said Yzelda could leave at three. I bought hard rolls and cookies and told Yzelda to meet us at the plaza.

When I saw Divina, I told her I wanted to draw her, and asked her to wear her white blouse with the birds embroidered at the neck. She put it on with her white skirt, undid her braids, and brushed her hair back into a simple ponytail. She was cheerful—pleased, I could see, to be out for the afternoon, and pleased, too, that we were a party of friends.

"Will you swim?" she asked Riley when she saw him. He was dressed in jeans.

"It will be too cold," I said. "But it's a lovely spot to see."

"Another time we'll go to the mineral baths, if you want," Riley said. The baths were on the road between Tecatitlán and Lago. "I haven't been there yet myself."

On the highway, Divina and Yzelda sang Beatles songs in the back seat. Divina was teaching the words to Yzelda, who couldn't quite get her tongue around the English words, and often dissolved into laughter. Once, Riley turned around and sang along for part of the song about Strawberry Fields, but Divina knew it better.

"How do you know those old songs?" he asked her.

"The tapes show up in the market. Who knows? Left behind, passed around." She shrugged. "Who cares? They play. I like them."

"Me too," he said.

We parked half a mile from the road, where the Jeep wasn't visible to those on the highway. I had brought a small basket with the bakery goods and a pineapple, a knife, and a jar of strawberry jam. I gave Riley a big bottle of mineral water to carry. We climbed over the bank, and saw, as I had remembered, a kind of staircase of natural basins going up the gorge. They were small and not deep, but very pretty, with shrubs and trees close around, and many pockets of deep shade, with open sunny spots where it was pleasant to sit. At the top of the climb there was a trickle of water that fell down over the rocks and splashed into the pool. At other times of the year, there would be a considerable waterfall for a while. We stopped at the first basin, where there was the greater expanse of flat ground and foliage.

The girls were almost bouncing with excitement. "Go on, take a look around," I said. "Let Riley and me settle in, and then I'll do some drawing." I had brought a blanket, and I spread it out in the sun and lay on my side, propped on my elbow. Riley leaned against a big flat rock.

"I'd like to send Divina some new tapes when I get home," he said. "My nephew Derek could pick them. She'd like that, wouldn't she?"

"Does an enchilada have sauce?" I answered. Then I asked, "Is everything okay at home? In Chicago, I mean."

"Why do you ask?"

I hoped he wouldn't think I was prying. "In the village they say, The gringo is important. He receives so many calls from the States. The girl in the office says, pooh, there is a wife back there, wondering when is he coming home."

He winced. "My sister Margaret was calling me every other day. It was embarrassing, the little boy running up the hill to tell me, 'The lady called again, Señor.' She said the way I talked worried her, what was I not telling her? I didn't tell her all my plans, that's what was bothering her. She doesn't understand a trip without a schedule and a guide. I don't want her to worry, but I'd had enough."

"What did you say?"

"That it's my vacation. That I'm going to stay for fiesta, and then I'll come home. I didn't say how soon that is. Or how much I hate to leave. I told her not to call the village anymore, that I wouldn't call back. I'm sure it was a shock."

He seemed pleased with himself.

"You could settle in here easily enough for the winter. Already I see the villagers greet you familiarly. We could find you a place."

"You told me I wasn't old enough for your writing class. Well, I'm neither old enough nor rich enough for retirement or extended vacations. And I miss home. I miss my dogs, and the store. I miss my neighbors. I was thinking—when I'm home, some Saturday morning I'll wake up and hear voices from the yard next door, below my window, and I'll think I'm here. I'll get up and be surprised to remember that I'm in Chicago. They'll be speaking Spanish, and playing tapes they bought in Guadalajara. Felipa will be cooking something that smells delicious. I love my neighborhood." He bit his lip.

"What else? You're working up to saying something, aren't you?"

"You can go back and forth so easily," he said. "For the price of a ticket."

"So come back," I said.

"A person who had ties here could return often. It wouldn't be like leaving India."

"I see." I could feel a request for advice coming. *Ask her.* What else could I suggest?

But just then the girls came down into our sunny spot and plopped themselves down. Their skirts billowed and fell around them like petals. Divina said, "It's a good bird place, I can tell. I wish I had my trap." She said to Riley, "You haven't eaten my chile quail. It's delicious."

"I hope I can," he said.

"There," I said, gesturing to the girls. "Sit together, like sisters, you know? Lean your heads together."

Riley lay back and closed his eyes. The girls relaxed into a pose, and I concentrated on my sketching. Except for a long plume of birds that passed overhead, we were quite alone. None of us spoke for most of the next hour. When I had made several drawings, I sighed audibly, set down my pad, and said, "Everybody stretch while I get out the food."

Riley asked to see the drawings. One was of Divina alone, a three-quarter profile. Exposed by the cut of her blouse, her long neck made an elegant line. I liked it. "What do you think?" I asked Riley. He touched the edge of the paper and said nothing.

The girls came around to look. Yzelda was the more delighted, because it was new to her. "Do I look like that?" she demanded. "Do I really?" Divina laughed and kissed Yzelda's cheek. "You can have it, sweetie," I told Yzelda. She clapped her hands.

Riley suggested cutting the pineapple on the rock. "So it won't get on the blanket," he said. It was a plump, juicy, big fruit. As soon as he broke it open, the ripe sweet smell struck us and we all declared we were hungry. I passed around the rolls and jam, which we ate sitting on the blanket, and then we all stood and took pieces of the pineapple. Juice ran onto our chins and forearms. We laughed and licked and wiped, but we were a mess.

Riley went over to the basin and bent to wash his hands.

"Come on to the upper tub," Yzelda said. "You have to see how pretty it is."

I took up the blanket and we followed her past a second basin to the third, where the water fell and made a little foam. It splashed over a high rock, out from it so that you could almost stand behind the falling water. I washed, then spread the blanket.

Divina said, "Oh, look, my hair is sticky, too." She stood close to the streaming water and washed her arms and splashed her face, and then bent forward and lifted her ponytail around to wash the tip.

"How did you get your hair sticky?" Yzelda asked. She was crouched at the pool, timidly taking up water in the cup of her hand. I sat on the edge and put my feet in, pulling up my skirt and baring my knees. The water was cold, and I wished the weather were hot enough to swim nude. I promised myself I would sometime. Riley had stooped and washed quickly and was done. He stood away from us, turned to look out at the vista. From here you could see across the highway where the mountains rolled away.

Divina stepped in closer to the cold falling water, laughing and splashing herself. Suddenly, with a quick shriek, she slid on a rock. She didn't fall, but she had stepped far enough forward that the water streamed over the front of her, soaking her face and blouse and a lot of the front of her skirt. She was laughing as she stepped back. She undid her ponytail and shook her head like a puppy. She lifted her head to the sun and stretched out her arms to shake off the water.

Her face was golden in the sun. Her wet hair streamed down her back; pieces of it lay on her neck and over her shoulders. Her wet blouse clung to her breasts and abdomen, their whiteness muted by the undertone of flesh.

"Oh, Divina!" Yzelda cried softly, her hands lifted to her mouth.

Divina stood still. Slowly she put her arms down at her side in a long, fluid motion. She arched her back, just for a moment, in an easy stretch, like a cat. She looked past me, toward the mountains. She was smiling. She was radiant.

She was looking at Riley. His was the face of an astonished man. I had a crazy thought that he might step backwards and fall, but he didn't move a muscle. I looked back at Divina, and saw her as I knew Riley did—not the girl who had run off giddily to explore with Yzelda, not that at all—

but a self-possessed young woman who had just struck a man with the force of her beauty.

Oh, God, for a camera! I thought, but I would not forget.

I pulled the blanket up from the ground, and ran to her.

A
Candle Burns

DIVINA WAS SO QUIET AT SUPPER, her mother leaned across the table to feel her forehead. "Were you in the sun too long?"

Divina said she was tired.

"Was it pleasant at the pool?"

"Yes, Mama, very pleasant."

"And did Charlotte draw?"

"Yes, Mama." Divina jumped up and ran from the patio into the house.

When Consolata had cleaned the dishes, she went in and sat on Divina's bed. Divina lay on her stomach, her arms flung out, her face turned to the wall.

"Are you ill?"

"No, Mama, no."

Consolata sat a few more minutes, her hand on her daughter's arm.

She said, "Good night, child," without a trace of impatience.

Divina said, "Not a child, Mama. I'm almost nineteen years old."

Consolata smiled, though Divina couldn't see. "You will always be my child, love. But you are a woman, too. Anyone can see that."

Later, Divina washed her face and went out to her mother's hut. Though her mother lay in the dark, she heard her daughter coming, and got up to light the lamp. Divina crawled up onto her mother's bed and sat beside her.

"Tell me," her mother said. And Divina did.

When Divina went back into the house, she took with her a candle from her mother's altar, and a small jar with sweet oil. She took off her clothes. She tipped the jar to wet her fingers, and touched her body with the oil in many places. She rubbed her nipples, the lobes of her ears, the flesh around her navel. Her eyes were shut. She pulled her head back. Her long hair fell to the mattress and spilled on the sheet.

She capped the jar and set it on the table, and pulled on a cotton gown. She lay under the sheet and watched the flickering shadows as the candle burned. When morning came, her mother went to the phone office and called the hotel to say that Divina was ill and could not come in. By then Divina was already gone, up to the hills above the village, where she could walk until her legs ached and her mind was clear.

She took her bird trap with her.

PART THREE

In Which a Soul Is Tormented,
a Painting Unveiled,
and a New Tale Begins

Tangy
Birds

DIVINA KNEW A PLACE IN THE HILLS where a small spring flowed all year and there was sweet grass in an alcove of rocks and flowering bushes. She set her trap and lay down to doze in the pale morning sun. In her long red skirt and a yellow T-shirt, she looked like a tropical flower.

Riley woke restless, and set off on an ambitious hike. By eight he was hot and thirsty and hungry, irritated with himself for his poor planning—all he'd carried was a banana, gone in a gulp—but exhilarated, too, by the fresh breeze and the views. He passed a man on a burro, and a child leading a goat on a rope. At moments the air seemed riotous with birds, then there would be silence. Sometimes he heard voices, but never saw the speakers.

Divina stirred as the sun went behind a cloud. She opened her eyes and saw that it was Riley making the shadow—the sky was still clear—and she sat up unstartled, as if she had been expecting him all along.

She had brought with her several small local fruits—some like crabapples, another looking like an ugly big kiwi—and she took them out of her pocket and offered to share them with Riley. He sat near her on the ground. "I am hungry," he said. The sun on his hair made it glint red. His face was glossy with perspiration. He took out his handkerchief and patted his forehead.

Divina wiped the little apples on her skirt. They were crisp and very sour, but Riley and Divina ate them with pleasure. She cut open the ugly fruit. It was a pale green and prickly, studded inside with soft seeds in a jellylike flesh, and it tasted like grass. Riley made a face, and Divina laughed and gave him another bite off her knife. "Aiee," he said, making her laugh, but he ate it.

She showed him the spring and bent to take a drink from her cupped hand. He hesitated, put his hands in the water, then splashed his face. They knelt to check the trap. Four little birds huddled in a corner. Divina took them out one by one. He watched closely as she wrung their necks and set them on the ground. The last, still alive, she handed to Riley. It was hot and pulsing in his palm. It didn't make a sound. She laid the three dead birds in the cage. He handed her the last, with an audible sigh, and she killed it in a single motion, and put it in the cage, too.

"Have you never hunted?" she asked.

"Never."

"Nor caught a bird?"

"Never."

"Then you must come this afternoon to help me clean them. I will hang them. And then we'll cook, okay?"

He nodded his head yes. "So the famous chile quail begins like this." He laughed. "All my meat has come from a cold case in the supermarket. And never quail. I've never tasted it."

"It's so tasty, you'll see."

"Here, let me carry the cage."

As she handed it to him, she said, "I didn't notice before how red your hair is."

He gave his head a pat. "You should see my sister Margaret. She's what they call a carrot top. And her son Derek, too."

"Carrot top." Divina repeated the English phrase intently. She brightened. "Orange!"

"That's right. I don't even think of myself as a redhead. I'd have said sandy."

She knew a path that led directly into the village. He walked behind her, not half as agile as she on the uneven ground. As they came onto a street, she took the cage and said, "I and my little quails will wait for you, Tom Riley."

"I look forward to it," he said.

She said, "I know."

At a cafe on the square, Riley ate a breakfast of beans and eggs and coffee, then went to the schoolhouse. On the grounds in the back were various floats in progress for the fiesta. There were washtubs full of cut crepe paper for the decorations, and the older children—eight, nine years old— were draping and stapling and gluing. To one side was the structure for the huge fireworks explosion that would take place when it was dark, before the dance. It was impossibly built with towers, wheels, and sticks like the branches of trees. "Could you use a hand?" he called. The men waved to him to come over. One by one they shook his hand. Someone gave him the end of a long slat, and he moved where they told him to place it.

*   *   *

Divina took the bus into Lago de Luz in order to go to the big market there. She carried the basket Riley had bought in the market after lunch, the day they went to Mary of Tears. She took a long time at the stalls of chiles and vegetables, peeling back the husks to inspect the kernels, tapping the cactus paddles for firmness. She sniffed the cilantro, and turned tomatoes all around. She moved on to cheeses, and asked for tastes, until she found one that was salty, sharp, and creamy. The vendor said, "It's only cheese, you know," and Divina bent forward to whisper, "It is a very special meal." She tilted her basket to show the chiles. The woman said, "Good luck, Señorita."

When she had everything she needed, she went by the Patio and drank an orange Fanta and waited for a free moment when her mother could hear what she had to say. They stood over by the cooler and talked quietly. Divina hugged her mother and left. She walked in long lithe strides, humming a song she was inventing, making her way to the bus stop.

As Riley approached the house late that afternoon, he could hear her singing on the patio. "Beside the water we found flowers," she sang. "Flowers of silk and satin, flowers of yellow gold." He went around the outside of the house and entered a back gate. She was still wearing her red skirt, but had changed to a sleeveless black blouse. Her hair was wound with a red ribbon through it, and pinned snugly at the back of her head. She had covered the table with newspaper, and set two bowls in the middle. The birds were strung up by their limp necks from hooks off of the roof. Nearby hung tubes tied with bright ribbons. The tubes dripped into a round shallow pan, a hummingbird feeder.

The first thing Riley noticed was the way the tiny quail feet curled under their bodies. He had brought beer, and he set it down on the cool stones by the door into the house.

Divina said, "You're just in time." She took a bird down from the hook and handed it Riley. "First we pick the feathers. Then we'll clean the cavities. There's nothing to it." He stroked the bird once, then began picking. Divina took another bird down and plucked all the feathers before he had cleared one side of his. She had started the last bird when he was done with his. She handed it to him and said, "Finish this one while I clean up a little of the mess." She scooped and brushed feathers into a pile in a sheet of the newspaper and folded and set it aside.

"Now we're ready to eviscerate them," she said. "Here, come watch." He stepped closer. She said, "Put your thumb under the breastbone—see right here—and hold the tail. You just break it, like this." Snap! and she had opened the bird; deftly, she slid in two fingers, and in a second motion, brought out the entrails.

"How did you do that!" he said in admiration.

"You'll see," she said. She handed him a bird and stood close by his arm. He tried to do just as she had done.

"Here—" She touched the bird. "Feel the point of the breastbone. That's it. Oh, you'll be running a bird stall in the market now, Mister Riley," she teased.

He felt his fingers along the bone. The bird had cooled since morning, but it didn't feel like something dead. It was more like it had never been alive. But he couldn't forget that he had seen them shivering in the cage. He managed to suppress a shudder. When he pulled out the innards, to his immense surprise, he felt a surge of pleasure, as if he had done something powerful or clever. *Heavens,* he thought. *Margaret should see me now.*

Divina stepped off the stones into the yard and held each bird away from her body and took off the head. Blood splattered on the dirt. She washed them inside and out in a pan of water and laid them in one of the bowls. Everything she did was expert, easy, and in some way beautiful to watch. The birds had a smell he didn't recognize—the smell of wildness, he supposed. He couldn't imagine eating them, but he knew he would.

Their hands were streaked with blood and feathers. It seemed a miracle that their clothes had not been stained. He looked around for something to wipe his hands on. "Wait," she said. "We'll wash." She went to the edge of the patio and dipped her hands in a bucket on the ground. She dumped it out and went out of sight, quickly reappeared, and carried the clean water over to the table. She pulled the newspaper out from under the bowls and twisted it into a paper log and laid it by the stove. She scooped a cup of water into the empty bowl, sloshed it around, and threw it out. "Give me your hands," she said, reaching for them. He held them out over the bowl.

She scooped water from the bucket and poured it over his hands again and again until the water ran clean from his fingers. The water was cool. She gently rubbed her finger across his cuticles, turned his hands, and wiped the palms. She took the bowl away and set the bucket aside. She took a cloth from a stool by the door and carefully dried his hands, then her own.

His heart was pounding.

She smiled at him and picked up the stripped birds. "My mother taught me that when you cook, the food is the whole world. It requires everything, and then, when you serve it, you get everything back." She wiped her forehead with the back of her hand.

"I could use a beer," he said. "What about you?"

"Could I have a sip of yours?" she asked.

Neither of them mentioned the absence of Consolata.

*   *   *

"Tell me about the meals that you remember," I sometimes say to my students. I don't give any more directions than that. It isn't necessary. Everyone remembers food and the rituals that surround it. Sometimes the writing is focused on the food itself, sometimes on the traditions the food celebrates, sometimes on the dynamics of the family. Men will name the dishes they have loved: their mother's apple dumplings, a wife's pot roast with onions; potato latkes browned just so. Women are more likely to talk about the preparation. "I always used butter," I've read. "We didn't know about cholesterol then. And it was butter that gave the flavor . . ." Sometimes it is the occasion that provides the focus. Thanksgiving dinners. Barbecues for Independence Day. Hot dogs at the beach. Sometimes the meals were terrible events. Father always got drunk, Auntie always cried. Once I read the sad memory a woman wrote of the day she realized she'd forgotten her recipe for chess pie, though she'd made it the week before. She wrote: "I knew I was old and nothing would be easy for me anymore."

Rarely is a single meal the subject of a student's musings. When it is, the most memorable ones turn out to be funny or awful. "It was our first dinner after the honeymoon. She forgot to put baking powder in the corn bread." "He sliced the ham, and then broke down and told me about the cancer."

Everyone has something to say about food, but hardly ever do they say what really happened when the meal took place. Who was loved, denied, favored, remembered? How was someone changed? How did the food carry the emotion from the cook to the diner? Maybe those things are carried too deep inside us for casual sharing. Maybe too deep to say in words.

Riley will remember the quail. How he watched as Divina rubbed them with coarse salt, lime, and the seeded inner flesh of long red chile pods. The smell of their skin as she charred them over a hot fire. After that she placed them in a clay pot and covered them to cook while they prepared the other dishes. There was a dish of avocado with pickled chiles. They laid corn in its husk on the charcoal fire to blacken. She directed him to chop cilantro and tomatoes and onions for the rice. They stopped to snack on cheese that crumbled in his hand, then melted in his mouth. He learned to hold the cactus paddles gingerly and remove the spiny nodes. She cooked them on the fire, then gave them to him to cut into strips. "My mother eats them twice a week, for the blood," she said. When he cut into them, they were tender and moist.

There was a hummingbird that came and went at the feeder. He watched it for long moments, mesmerized.

He helped her scrub the table down. They brushed the water off onto the patio stones and he swept it away. The blood washed away; there was only a pink glaze left in places. Divina brought out a red cotton cloth and threw it over the table, then set out earthenware dishes and plates of food. He opened another bottle of beer, and she rubbed glasses with lime and he poured it.

"Just a little while," she said. She sat between the table and the stove. He leaned back in a chair strung with braided rawhide strips. "Talk to me about the food," he said.

She spoke in Spanish, in a low, mellow voice. He didn't understand much of what she said; the vocabulary was strange to him. He didn't concentrate. He let the words spill over him like the water on his hands. He couldn't take his eyes off her. The black blouse fit snugly. Her bared shoulders shone. He admired her hair. He could not keep from think-ing of it. The way the ribbon was wound was a mystery. If she took it out her hair would spill over her shoulders. He had seen it free numerous times, and it hadn't mattered so much as now, when she hid it from him, tucked so primly in its whorl.

The feast filled the table. The delicious smells enveloped him. She handed him a basket, and when he peeled back the cloth, steam rose from hot tortillas and warmed his face. The flesh of the bird pulled away from the bone with a flick of the fork. It was moist and sharp and tender. They ate it with their fingers, and sucked the grease and juices from their own flesh. The yellow corn, released from its black jackets, was tough to the bite, then yielded sweetness in the kernel. He ate more messily than he ever had.

"Wonderful," he said. "Oh, this is good." They ate greedily at first, then slowly, savoring each bite. There was nothing more to say until they were satisfied. Once, the hummingbird darted between them in a long swooping dive, fluttered the ribbon on the feeder, then drank.

"We could take a walk," he said. "We could sit in the plaza." He could see that that pleased her. He wanted to be seen with her. He wanted the village to say, "There goes Divina with the gringo." He wished Margaret could see her. A crazy confidence was flowing in him.

They put their dishes into a large tin bowl, and she covered it with a cloth. She said, "Wait a moment," and went inside. Soon she came out and now her hair was brushed long, down her back. She had put on a necklace made of crocheted string, with a tiny stone at her throat.

Along the streets, the doors of houses were propped open. People sat on chairs on the walk, or even in the street. There seemed to be children everywhere. "Good evening," Divina said as she passed. "Good evening," Riley echoed. Their heels clicked on the stones. They passed a house where an old woman was leaning on her windowsill on her elbows. Lined up on either side of her were little packages of Chiclets, and wrapped chunks and strips of candy. He bought the things Divina pointed to. They turned out to be squash candy and candied melon strips, sweet as caramel.

She saw Yzelda coming down the street. "Just a minute," she told Riley, and ran to her friend to whisper and giggle and almost dance.

"Psst," the old woman said. "You, gringo."

"Me?" Riley said.

"You will marry her?"

He gasped.

The old woman leaned out and pointed to the sky. "Soon it will be dark, and girls do not stay skinny. You remember what I say. Don't leave her with her face hidden in her shawl."

"Oh, Señora," he exclaimed. "You misunderstand."

"Misunderstand what?" Divina asked, returning to his side.

"She thought I wanted more candy," Riley rushed to say. "But I couldn't eat another bite."

The woman cackled and pulled back, out of sight.

They passed the barbershop. It was full of children, two or three in each chair, and others on stools mugging in the mirror. Music was blaring from a radio. The happy barber was clipping the hair of a toddler who stared out to the street, solemn and still. A young woman stood in front of him, clapping her hands and bubbling with delight. A first cut? Riley wondered. A big day.

They passed a circle of little girls singing and dancing in a circle. One child was outside, darting at the circle, trying to gain entry.

"What are they singing?" he asked. "It isn't Spanish, is it?"

"It is older than Spanish," Divina said. "You see how the girls dance close together? They are defending the girl inside."

Only now did he see the girl in the middle. "Defending her from what?"

"She's the little nun, and no man can have her," she said. They walked on. "Let me see if I can tell you the words:

> *"Sweet orange, celestial lemon,*
> *"Tell Maria not to lie down . . ."*

In the plaza they sat on a cool stone bench and watched the villagers out for the evening. All around, vendors' kiosks were in various states of preparation for the fiesta. The place had the look of a county fair. A teenage boy was selling balloons. Riley bought three and tied the strings together and gave them to Divina. She held them as they talked. An old woman walked by pushing a rusty wheelbarrow piled with tattered paperback books and comic strip novels. She stopped in front of them. Divina shook her head and the woman moved on.

"I saw books in your house," he said. "In English and Spanish both. They are yours?"

"I read every night," she said. "My brother says, 'I'll buy you a television,' but we told him, for what? To hear loud people acting silly? To watch old American shows? I would rather read. Sometimes I read to my mother."

"How long did you go to school?"

"Six years," she said. He could hear the pride in her voice.

"And every child doesn't," he guessed.

"No. There were only two of us that stayed that long among the students our age. Antonio was the son of a pharmacist in Lago. He went on to secondary school. Now he studies medicine at the university in Guadalajara."

"And you—did you want to go to secondary school as well?"

"Yes, why not?"

"And school is free?"

She laughed. "Free? There are always fees. Uniforms. Books.

I went to the school in Lago to see. They said sometimes a student is sponsored. I put my name down. I took tests. They let me come for the first two weeks. Math and literature, science. I was so excited. But all the students sponsored were boys. My brother sent money home, but we were saving for my mother's cafe. 'Go, you must go,' she said. But I knew she wanted me to be a teacher, and I didn't know if I could do that. I didn't think I would like it. I want a family of my own, not other people's children. And to study with no plan in mind? It's a luxury for rich girls. I said I didn't like the school."

"So you went to work."

"My teacher—she would have been my teacher—said she needed someone in her house. I worked for her two years. I looked after her babies. Many nights I stayed there, and she brought books home from her classroom for me. When I came home to the village at night, I brought a book to study. I told my mother about other countries, and the stars, and the way an engine works. I taught her to read and write. Because of the teacher, I studied anyway, and because I had learned, my mother learned, too. Then the teacher said she didn't need me anymore; a relative was coming from her village to live with them. She knew an American family. They hired me and I was there a year. Then I left."

"They moved away?"

"Not until later. But I couldn't stay. The father looked at me in a way I understood would go somewhere I didn't want to follow. My mother said I should work at a hotel. There would be set hours, and I could find other things to do. That was when I began sitting for Charlotte."

"The painting. What is it like?"

"It's a girl dreaming."

"What do you think she dreams?"

Divina looked at him with surprise. "I know what she dreams, because I am the girl."

"Will you tell me?"

She was fiddling with the balloon strings, holding her arm up to let the spheres float higher. She pulled them back, her hands in her lap. The balloons almost looked like they were sitting on her shoulder. "I dream of a white house. Babies on a rug. Jacaranda trees in blossom." She shrugged. "There are no words for some dreams, are there? What do you dream?"

He was caught off guard. "Sometimes I dream of pyramids, a long river."

"Egypt!" she said.

"I suppose it is. A dream of a journey. And sometimes I am flying. Sometimes I dream of my wife, Eva."

"You had no babies?"

"My wife—she could not—" He reached across and batted a balloon. Divina laughed, surprised.

"I have my animals," he said. "At work. I like it, every day, to go into the shop and see so much life. It's the only work I've ever done. And then I come home and there are my dogs, so happy to see me, as if I have been gone a long time."

"Let me see the photographs again. Do you have them with you?"

He drew out snapshots of the dogs from his wallet. Shyly, he passed them to her.

"He looks so silky," she said of his small dog Sweetly.

"She," he said. "She is. When you talk to her, she tucks her head and looks at you so intently. I find myself speaking to her earnestly, as if she understands."

"She probably does," Divina said. She handed back the pictures. "But still you are lonely."

"I have my nephew and niece. Derek is living with me while he goes to school. And I am a godparent." He looked in his wallet again and handed her a snapshot of Oscar's granddaughters. It was a school portrait from the fall. They were third graders now. "Elise and Elena," he said.

Divina touched their faces. "They're Mexican."

"Many of my neighbors are. Nearby there are Mexican grocery stores, cafes, a place to buy music."

She stood up. "Still you are sad."

"No," he said. He meant not right now.

She lifted her arms as high as she could and let the balloons float away. Most of the children were gone, but one saw the balloons and shouted to his father, "Catch them!" which made the adults laugh. The father scooped his son up and said, "Catch you!"

As they walked back, she told him, "I learned a lot in the American house. They like their houses to have no smell. It's very odd. I was always spraying one smell to cover up another. I can cook their food. Macaroni and cheese. Spaghetti and meatballs. Fried chicken. I can make the devil's food cake, too."

"Those foods are nothing compared to what you made tonight."

"You liked it?"

"Very much."

He hesitated at the house. "Let me help you," he said. It was night now. Families had gone indoors, children were in bed. She took him through the house, turning on the light and a lamp on a shelf. Outside there was a bulb over the table. She pulled a small bucket near them and threw scraps into it. He handed her dishes and after she emptied them, she put them into a pile to wash. She made a fire and put water on to boil. He sighed; he knew he should go.

He stepped toward the gate as she stepped toward him. Their shoulders bumped lightly. He could feel the cool night air, but his face was hot. His shoulder, where she had touched him, throbbed. "Your mother—" he said. His voice came out crackly.

"She is with the women tonight. They are praying a rosary for Tía Filomena."

"What will your neighbors say?" He was now acutely conscious of the evening as others would see it. Had he compromised her in some way? The villagers would gossip. He thought of the woman in the window.

"They will say—" He smelled something minty in her hair. He felt the warmth of her arm a hair's breadth away from his. "They will say, 'When will the gringo go home?'" she whispered. "They will say, 'When it was night, the lights came on,' and they will sigh in disappointment."

"Divina." His breath was ragged. He wanted to kiss her. *My God*, he thought. *This*, he thought, *is what it is like to be enchanted.*

She whispered, "I have many skills, Thomas. I can cook and sew. I can walk all day over rough ground. I'm strong. I can learn whatever I need to."

He took her hands and stepped back so that their arms were outstretched. "You are a splendid cook!" he said, much too loudly. "I thank you, oh, it was a wonderful meal, I'm so sorry Consolata wasn't with us." He backed into the table. "Oh!" he cried. He'd struck his leg with the sharp corner. "Oh!"

She wasn't quite smiling. She was fiddling with the amulet on her neck. "I know a hundred songs."

"Good night, good night," he said. He went out through the gate and hurried away clumsily. He made such a clatter, the old woman Imelda leaned out of her window to see who was drunk. When she saw who it was, she turned around and spoke to Consolata. "He's gone." She sat down on her bed and began to laugh; she laughed so hard, she fell over.

*   *   *

Divina takes her time washing up. She hums a Beatles song: "Falling, yes I'm falling . . ."

It isn't long before Consolata comes home. Divina makes a chocolate drink for them. She beats it in a bowl and pours it, peaked with froth, into cups.

An
Agitated Soul

RILEY FINDS HIS BALANCE AGAIN. He is nearly bouncing on the cobblestones, making his way up the hill to Pete's house. He doesn't notice the villagers leaning out of their windows, or the night watchman Rogelio, who turns onto the street just behind him and shakes his head. Rogelio has never seen the gringo like this. Maybe it's something about *norteamericanos* that they get happy when they're drunk. He himself is a weeper. When he sees the worm at the bottom of the bottle, he knows where his life is headed. How short it is. He wishes he had some of what the gringo has been drinking.

Pete is watching basketball from Detroit. He offers Riley a beer.

Riley sits down as if this were an evening like any evening. The basketball game makes no sense at all. Men running from one end of a court to the other. Balls in hoops. Shouting. It's as if he's never seen a game. As if he's from another planet. He can't sit still. He drinks the beer and feels it go down his body to make a cool place in his belly.

When the ads come on, Pete says, "Great day, Riley! The phone truck came at last, and we've got service. The showers are functioning. The fireworks wheel is going to be ready in time. And I called my wife and she's leaving at six in the morning."

"Leaving where?"

"I didn't tell you? She's coming for a week's vacation. What do you think—will she like the house? There's still a lot to finish, but our bedroom is done. I did that room first."

"The house is wonderful. Pete, is this too nosy—I thought you must be separated from your wife. Is this a reconciliation?"

"Oh, no, it's not like that. My Cindy is a modern woman. She's the manager of the crafts and fabrics department of a Wal-Mart, and she's got eleven months to go till retirement. I told her I wanted to go to Tecatitlán, and she said, 'So go, but not me, I want my own check.' At first I said I'd put off coming down, but we talked about it, and it made sense. I come down and get the house, make it habitable—she's never spent a night in this village. All those years we came to see my mother, she stayed in a hotel in Lago when she came. I'll go back and forth, a few months here, a few months there. Then we'll both go back and forth. Till then, why not? We don't have a lot of unfinished business, after thirty years. A little time apart's not bad. She can trust me. I've never been a sport. You know what I mean."

"I'm glad she's coming now. For fiesta."

"A whole week with a wife, whooee!" He lifts his beer toward the ceiling. "Her Spanish is sooo bad."

Riley is grinning. "That's wonderful. I know what you mean." He blushes scarlet. He does think he knows what Pete means.

Pete says, "It's not my business. But I've come to like you a lot. You aren't going to get old all by yourself, are you?"

"I thought there couldn't be anyone after Eva."

"She's gone. Sad but true."

"I know, but I thought she was—I don't know how to say this—I thought she was my fate."

"Thought? Is that widow Arispe changing your mind?"

Riley gulped.

"We're friends here, aren't we?" Pete says. "I'm not out of line?"

"No. It's that I don't know what I want. I don't know."

"Why, pin a tail on a burro, you're in love, aren't you?"

"Can something real happen so fast?"

Pete hopped up. "Hell, this calls for more beer. And I just had a case delivered. Turn that damned machine off. I'll put on music. Frank Sinatra? Perry Como? You say."

"Take what's on top, so you don't have to make a decision."

They drank more beer before they went to bed. Pete ran out of things to say and lapsed into his own reverie. Riley sat in his chair and pondered his excitement and fear. It was way past midnight when he said to Pete, "She's just so beautiful. I watched her hands tonight. Those long fingers. Hard as she works, you wouldn't think she'd have that kind of delicacy. So beautiful."

"Don't mind me saying this, but I never saw it, myself. She's a nice lady. And looks aren't everything. They're not a nickel to the dollar of a person's character. And Consolata has character. But pretty? I'd never have said that."

Riley couldn't look at him.

"Say. You don't mean—hell, you mean the girl! Divina!"

"Did you know she speaks English?"

"Yeah, she speaks English. You old dog. What do you

know? She's beautiful, all right. And cool as an iced *cerveza*. Nobody gets near her."

"Do you think I'm too old? Is it crazy?"

"Are you kidding? You're a damned catch, Riley. You're not old. Hell, you're not retired yet."

"I do need to get home."

"So what about her?"

"I don't know. It's all so new. If I misunderstood—what a fool—"

"You don't know what her feelings are?"

"I'm not a very experienced man."

"None of us are Kevin Costner here."

"But she said things to make me think—she might—care—"

"What did she say?"

"I can't remember! I remember the smells. Chiles and lime juice. Mint in her hair. Garlic on our breath."

Pete looked ready to cry. "This is so damned romantic."

"Let's see what I feel like in the morning," Riley said. "Let's see what Divina says."

He tried to sleep. He might have had a fever, the kind that makes you happy. He saw flashes of a future. A crib in his old room. The two of them dancing in the street during the neighborhood fair. He saw—he saw her bare shoulder, and her back, the curve of it down to her hips. He put his hand on her back gently, knowing he would slide it around to her breast.

Oh, God, he prayed. *Don't let me sin.*

He slept.

He dreamed. He was in an open field and the sky was rent with lightning. He dreamed he was afire but not consumed, dancing in the field and crying out like a madman. He had been there before, he knew that. Eva! he cried in his dream, but she wasn't there.

He woke and sat up abruptly. He had forgotten Eva. He had forgotten to speak to her, to say good night. He hadn't even looked at her photograph.

He turned on the bedside lamp and reached for the picture.

Really, Riley, he could hear her saying. *What do you think you're up to?* Maybe he was hearing Margaret instead.

He was so confused! Happy—giddy, really—and yet dreaming dreams of hell. Wasn't that hell? To burn and never stop? Or was that passion?

What did he have to compare it to? He had loved Eva. Her wit and erudition. Her efficiency and ingenuity. Her kindness and grace. The comfort of her company. The way she nudged him toward a better self.

And there had been that other part. To touch her sometimes. She would turn to him and draw him to her breast. She would give herself, a gift. It was so special, to be with her. He had told himself it wasn't meant to happen often. He came to her grateful. He might have missed the solace of a woman's body, if not for her.

Divina. He thought of her running across the field to him, leaping into the fire. He thought of her in his house. He thought of her stepping out of her bath. He thought of her in the kitchen, leaning over to give him a taste from her spoon. He would give her necklaces for her long throat. Bright stones on silver chains. Onyx beads and milky pearls. And when she cooked, he would stand at the counter beside her, he would chop and stir; he would wash the bowls she used. Sometimes they would take ice cream to bed while they watched TV.

He was going crazy.

He looked at the photograph again. In the background, behind the fountain, there were other figures. In the haze of out-of-focus, two girls strolled arm in arm. One might have been Divina. A girl when he married Eva. A child.

He was too disturbed to sleep. He got up and went into the kitchen to find something cool to drink. An orange soda. He took it into the dark salon and sat on the window seat looking out on the gardens. The moon was nearly full, milky as an opal behind a scrim of clouds. The flowers on the bushes shimmered.

"Someone else can't sleep," Pete said behind him. He pulled over a chair. There they were, two middle-aged men in Sears cotton pajamas. They both saw it at the same time, and started laughing.

"What are you going to do?" Pete asked.

"I'm going to find a way to save my soul," Riley answered.

In her house, Divina is sleeping. She dreams, too—as fiercely as Riley—but she doesn't wake. She enters the dream as into a pool. Beside her tonight sleeps her mother. Around the room they have lit candles and dishes of herbs.

The village dreams: of lost goats and old lovers, of dead children and the green promise of spring.

The village sleeps, but there is the moon to light Riley's way. He walks down the hill to the square, and across to the chapel. In the priest's house, there is a lit lamp.

Riley finds the chapel door ajar. The moonlight enters through the door, through the high windows on that side, through the glass above the altar. On one of the benches that have backs, near a statue of the Madonna with her child, the priest sits. Riley coughs lightly and sits beside him.

The priest speaks as if they have been sitting together all along. He gazes at the statue and he says, "When I was much younger, I confused love and passion, then I confused contrition and despair. I confused God with judgment, and fled to a place where I thought he might be gentle. But the village has taught me about God. Taught me how to speak of him, to speak of his absence and our terror and sorrow and pain. How, all the while, I know he will choose us in ways we don't predict, and love us in ways we don't earn.

"I was sitting here thinking that I have been waiting for the wrong things. I wanted God to flood my soul as the Nile floods Egypt. I thought there was a dry season and a season of the river, and I would wait until it rose again, and that was when I would feel his presence in my soul. I would pray and feel answered. Instead God plays a joke on me. He sends grace where I cannot reach for it. He sends me longing and I cannot feed it. And as soon as I see that, he plays his joke on me again, and what I thought I had to hide from becomes the very thing I should have sought—feeling. And if part of the feeling is joy, and part of it is sadness, still there is God in all parts of feeling."

"What if the feeling is so big and so new you can't judge it? How do you know if God sent it?" Riley kneaded his hands, then clasped his knees to stop the nervous motion.

"When God sends love where there are no obstacles, he means for you to embrace it, Riley," the priest says.

"I couldn't sleep. I tossed like someone on a raft. And I wanted to feel all of it. I couldn't resist it."

"Love is most perfect when the soul is sparked with agitation."

"I dreamed we were naked in a fire. Was it hell? Was the dream a sin?" Riley's voice quavers.

"Love, embraced as sacrament, is another face of God."

"You may not understand," Riley says. "You may not know who it is that disturbs my dreams."

"It is Consolata's daughter," the priest says. "We have all been watching you move toward her."

"Consolata—"

"She, most of all."

"I don't know if I believe that."

"Then you must ask her."

"And Eva."

"Mrs. Riley?"

"I was happy once. Then she died and I was bereft. How quickly my heart swells now! Am I so easily wooed from sorrow? Am I a shallow man?"

"God's love flows to low places," the priest says. "Go home, go to bed, go to sleep. Tomorrow is fiesta. They will bring the Virgin from across the valley for a week, to celebrate her love. Why shouldn't we celebrate yours as well?"

"Let me say a prayer first, Father. Pray with me, if you will. Pray that it isn't a dream after all."

"You won't know until you look at it in the light."

"I won't know until I see Divina again."

They walk out together and stand in the courtyard for a moment to look at the moon. They pray as men have prayed for millennia, in silent awe. It has nothing to do with words.

Morning
Light

HE SAT IN PETE'S GARDEN IN THE MORNING and drank coffee with
sweet condensed milk. A gardener on a rickety stepladder
was cutting oranges in the orchard. One of the papaya trees
had just come into bloom, and there were hummingbirds at
the flowers. In a birdbath, a tiny fountain bubbled.

"I've been meaning to ask someone," Riley said. "Why is
the fountain in the plaza dry? Was there ever water?"

"Yes, for many years. I heard the story of the fountain as
a child. There is an aqueduct to feed it. The soldiers wrecked
the pipes, above the town. For many years there was talk of
repairing it, but there is never money."

"What would it take?"

Pete shrugged. "Mostly, it's labor. Nobody has bothered
to look into it recently."

"Would you investigate it, when you have time? I would
like to see the fountain flow."

"What a good idea, Riley. And you know, there are a handful of villagers who could afford to make a contribution. I could."

"And me," said Riley. He set his cup down with a sigh.

"Short night, huh?" Pete said. But he was smiling. Cindy was due into Guadalajara in the afternoon.

"I'm off to Lago. Wish me well."

"To see Divina?"

"Consolata."

"Ah, of course."

"Later, Divina."

Pete put his hand out and shook Riley's. "A young wife will give you children and a long life, Riley."

"She would have to leave her home. Her mother. For me. I haven't asked her yet. What if I'm wrong?"

"Then she'll say no and we'll drink the rest of the beer. You better get out of here. You want a ride?"

"No, I like the bus. It gives me time to get myself ready."

As it did.

When he got to the Patio, he found Consolata alone, preparing food. Beans were bubbling in a large pot, and the counter was piled with produce. On a plate, blood leaked from a large brown paper package.

She smiled when she saw him. "Good morning."

"Could I speak to you?"

"Of course. Do you want coffee? It's almost ready."

"No, I had some. I only want to talk. No one will come this early?"

She smiled again. "Only you, Riley."

"Could you sit down with me for a moment?"

She came from behind the counter and wiped her hands down the front of her apron. "Let's sit outside. Here, help me with a table."

They pulled a table and chairs out next to a tree that had split the walk years before. She put her folded hands on the table. *She is so serene,* he thought. *She knows so much.*

"You look tired," she said when he didn't speak.

"I couldn't sleep. I was thinking back over this short time in the village. It is like a new life, bigger than the days that held it."

"Life is in the day I'm living," she said. "The rest is gone."

"My friendship with you has meant so much."

"Yes," she said.

"I had become bound up in my grief. I had forgotten how to be a friend."

"This happens," she said.

"And then I found myself thinking: What does a lonely man need but companionship? What does a sad man need but consolation?"

"Tomás?" She opened her hands and put them, palms down, on the table. "I am more comfortable saying Tomás. When Divina and I speak of you, we say 'Tomás.' Do you mind?"

"It is a beautiful name in Spanish. I never thought of how it would sound."

"I think I know what you were thinking. You and I—we have become friends, no?"

"I have felt content with you. Every day, I have looked forward to seeing you."

"But did you think—do you think—that I am alone?"

He knew suddenly that she was not. Embarrassed, he stammered, "I—I am alone."

"And you dreamed of a woman in the house, for company?"

"You make it sound foolish."

"You are looking at your own life with one eye closed. With your hands clasped like a monk."

Indeed, his hands were clenched so tight the knuckles were white. "Consolata." He spoke slowly. "What I feel for you—" He knew he was red-faced, but he had to say it. "It is like what I felt for Eva, and I thought, It had to be right. I was happy. And so I found myself hoping—wondering— would you ever think of leaving the village. All this—" he hastened to add—"before I thought of your life, and not just the part I'd seen."

She was smiling, waiting.

"And I was fond of Divina. I admired her. I thought of her as a girl."

"I know. There is not a day, a moment, when a girl becomes a woman. Even a mother fails to see it at first."

"But for me there was such a moment! And what I feel now—" He couldn't say.

"You could have a family, Tomás. We would all be a family. A border would not tear us apart." She raised her chin. "I know how to write."

"Divina wants this?"

"You must speak to her. It isn't for a mother to say."

"I'm so nervous! I want to find her right now. At the hotel, in front of everyone."

"No. Think about it. She would be there with her mop and uniform. What would you be doing? Rescuing her? Better, you will see her in the village, where she is no one's servant. Tonight she will be at the dance. She will be beautiful and happy and among friends. She will be her best self. Speak to her there."

"Of course." He felt the tension draining from his hands. "Oh, Consolata, do you think this is possible?"

"Tomás Riley. Listen. We are used to old gringos with

nothing to do but poke around our markets and our churches. You are a young man. And you are a *norteamericano.*

Riley understood that she spoke out of myth.

She said, "You have everything you need, except a wife and children. Birds do not curse you. Why shouldn't you live forever?"

The Envoy

GUESTS WERE LINGERING OVER LUNCH when the trio of young Americans showed up at the Posada Celestial. Brenda looked up from her plate of linguine and called to a waiter. "You didn't tell me the crab was fake," she complained.

"Where would we get crab here?" he asked insouciantly. He knew Señora Flaxman was fond of him. "Let me get you something else. A nice grilled flank steak?"

"Never mind," she said. "Who are they?" She pointed at the kids at the desk.

The waiter shrugged. "News to me," he said. His English was good. He planned to move to Guadalajara soon.

There were two men and a woman, all in their twenties. They wore backpacks, not too heavily loaded. The men were dressed in khaki shorts and T-shirts, the girl in a pretty cotton dress. The men had fashionable haircuts, long on top. One was a redhead, his hair worn lank and floppy. His dark-haired companion—Brenda guessed he was Thai, or Cambodian—wore his slicked sleek against his skull. He was also a walking jewelry store, with rings in his ears and his nose, and several chains around his neck. The woman was plump and almost pretty, with an old-fashioned curly hairdo and a sweet smile, in contrast to her friends' worried looks.

Brenda told Joe she'd be right back and went over by the desk as if she had just had a terrible urge to buy a postcard. She heard the redhead say he was looking for Tom Riley.

"He checked out some time ago," the clerk said. "I'd have to look—a week or more ago."

"I know, but don't you know where he went?" asked the redhead. His hair was an extraordinary orange color, and his face was full of freckles. He was quite darling, Brenda decided.

"No, sir. He didn't say. It was very sudden. We thought he went home."

"A village nearby. That's where he went. Do you know of it?"

"We have many villages in the lake region. What is it called?"

"I don't know. It must be very small. We had to call the phone office and leave a message so they could find him."

"This is the way the villages are," the clerk explained patiently. "Not everyone in Mexico has a phone."

"So tell us what's nearest. We'll start there. How far is near? What are we talking about here?"

"Going west, there's San Juan de Alma, three miles. Then Tecatitlán, and after that—"

"Excuse me," Brenda interrupted. "You're looking for Riley, aren't you?" She already knew this was going to be better than sitting around the pool all day.

The clerk bolted for the office where she could tell Señor Guttman, "It's about that gringo Riley."

Brenda put her hand out. "Brenda Flaxman. A friend of Riley's, I think I can say."

"Derek O'Malley," the redhead said. "Riley's my uncle. This is his stepdaughter Bernadette Wasierski, and my friend Trinh Bing. Do you know where my uncle is? Is there a place to stay there?"

"I'd take rooms here if you could," Brenda said. She wasn't going to let them get away. "He's bound to be in Tecatitlán. It's a very small place with nothing for tourists. Just what Riley was looking for, I'm guessing."

"But can I find him? You've seen him?"

"If he's in Tecatitlán, you can just sit down somewhere and wait for him to walk by."

"Truly?" asked Derek.

"Yes, today is fiesta. Everyone will be out. Say, why don't you check in and eat some lunch, and I'll dig us up a ride. I was thinking I'd go over later anyway. There's all the fiesta stuff, you know. Fireworks, dance."

Bernadette's smile grew larger. "I like to dance."

Trinh took her arm and gave her a twirl. "We'll show them how to do it, Bernie," he said.

Derek was calling for attention at the desk. Señor Guttman came out to help him. "How long would you be staying?" he asked stiffly.

"A few days, I suppose. Two rooms, have you got them?"

"And Mr. Riley, will he be returning?"

Brenda, behind them, said, "I wouldn't think so, would you, Guttman?" She stepped forward and put her arm over Derek's shoulder. "But I can vouch for these kids. I'm going to take them under my wing."

"Very good, Señora Flaxman," the manager said. To Derek, he said, "I can accommodate you with two small rooms on the street side. May I see your credit card?"

Derek took out his wallet. "I hope money will do," he said. "I'm not into plastic."

"Money is always good," the manager said. "As long as

you pay at registration. Fill out this form." He slid it across the counter.

"I was just wondering," Brenda said. "You know the pretty maid? Mr. Riley's friend?"

Señor Guttman was doing a poor job of suppressing his annoyance. "I'm not sure what you are asking me, Señora Flaxman."

"You know where she lives?"

"Certainly not."

"Tecatitlán, is it? I don't mean her doorstep, Guttman."

"I believe that is her village," he said. "If we are referring to the same employee."

Brenda laughed.

Guttman returned his attention to Derek. "Will you need help with bags?"

"Heavens, no." Derek's backpack wiggled. Brenda blinked. It wiggled again, and she caught a glimpse of silky black fur. She bit her lip to keep from asking what it was. It had to be a dog.

Guttman didn't see it. He laid the keys on the counter. "Welcome to the Posada Celestial," he said. "Welcome to Lago de Luz."

Charlotte stirred the sun-thickened linseed oil. It was like honey. She added amber Venice turpentine and shiny varnish.

She had pulled down the bamboo shutters to block the brightest light. She studied the painting of Divina. There was no denying it: She was done with the grisaille. She had to add color.

She took a deep breath and blew it out slowly with her eyes closed. Then she opened her eyes and began to mix the colors: the yellow ocher, vermilion, burnt umber, and on one edge, ultramarine blue for shadows, on the other, white for highlights. She had not mixed the flesh tones in years, but it came back to her without really thinking. She had loved this technique when she learned it in school. It had connected her to Ingres. And she had loved the long fore-play of the black and white, then the shift of energy with the tasks of glazing.

She had to work quickly. Keep her courage. This was the first glaze, the picture would no longer be black and white, but also not a real color. *Layers,* she told herself. *I have chosen to work in layers. I have chosen this way to work, and now I must do it.*

She began to paint. In a little while she was hot, and she took off the shirt she was wearing, stripping to her bra and undershirt. In a little while more she had worked up a sweat.

The painting could be ruined with color, she thought. Or made beautiful.

Work, she told herself. *Just work.*

Riley woke from a nap and showered. He was alone in the house. Pete had gone to pick up his wife. The maid was free for the fiesta.

He walked through the cool house with a towel wrapped around his hips. "I don't think you would be lonely for long," he practiced. "You would make many friends, I'm sure."

He stopped and examined his face in a mirror in the hall. He had shaved, and he ran his hand along the smooth flesh. "We will go to Spanish-language Mass. You will like our priest."

He shook his head and walked back to his room. She wouldn't need a lecture on life in Chicago. Hadn't she said she'd known the American family? Hadn't she heard him talk on and on about his neighbors, his dogs, his sister's family?

"Do you love me?" he tried.

His heart beat rapidly.

"I love you," he said.

He sat down on the bed.

"I will always be kind to you." No, he sounded like an employer.

"I will always love you." No, why else would he be proposing?

"Divina, would you marry me?"

He dressed. "Divina, would you marry me?" he said as he buttoned his shirt. "Marry me?" he said as he pulled on his pants. He tried singing it: "Marry, marry, marry me!" he trilled. He tried, "Will you be my wife?" but he liked the word "marry" best.

"Divina, Divina," he chanted, as he went out the door.

The villagers were casting ballots for fiesta princess. The voting was going on in the lobby of the tiny city hall. Outside, a small-bed truck announced the candidacy of "TERESITA, ANGEL OF TECATITLÁN." The truck was draped with cloth and tied all around with balloons. There was a white iron lawn chair on top of a wooden platform, with a striped umbrella stand. The pole was wrapped in tinfoil. Bouquets of fake pink flowers in baskets and handmade flags were placed about abundantly. A little boy in a white tuxedo was shouting, "Teresita, vote for Teresita."

Beside the truck was a small wooden cart, and in it two girls of primary school age sat on stools holding a crude banner that said, "OUR SWEETHEART IS SARITA." The girls were dressed in white lace dresses, with bright pink bows in their hair.

Riley peeked into the building. Behind a long table sat Don Genaro. On each side of him was a girl child no more than four years old. One was dressed extravagantly in tulle and satin, with a huge tinseled tiara that threatened to slide off her head at any moment. She was holding a wand speck-led with rhinestones, and smiling as expertly as a Miss Amer-ica back at home. On the other side, sweetheart Sarita was wearing a too-big white Communion dress she could have turned around inside of, and she looked scared enough to faint. In front of the children were scarred wooden boxes. A line of a dozen or more villagers snaked its way across from the door to the table. Each villager bought a ticket from Don Genaro, who deposited the coins in a large, noisy tin bucket. The villager then deposited the ticket in one of the little girls' boxes. So went the voting.

Riley couldn't bear to see it. He went outside again.

The streets around the plaza were full of vendors' booths, as at a fair. Everything imaginable was for sale. At one of the intersections, wooden rails and branches had been used to create an enclosed space in which little boys were racing around, taunting and ducking a young calf.

Riley strolled onto the plaza and walked around the foun-tain into the center.

Across the way, a woman was walking a tiny black and white dog. It looked so much like Sweetly, it made his heart ache. He walked a little closer.

"Riley, Riley!" the woman called, and threw her arms out.

"Bernadette!" Riley called back. The dog was now jump-ing straight up and down, like a yo-yo. "Oh, Sweetly," Riley cried. "My Sweetly." He hugged Bernadette, then knelt to pick up his dog.

"How in the world, Bernie? How did you get here?"

"On a plane," she answered. "I had an omelet in a little white dish."

"But not by yourself!"

She pointed, and Riley turned to see. At one of the benches, Derek was cutting a woman's hair. She had a towel draped around her shoulders, and was staring forward, as solemn as if she sat before a judge. Next to her a girl of thirteen or fourteen had her hair combed out like a drape over her shoulders and body, and another young man whom Riley had never seen before was carefully trimming the ends.

"Yo, Uncle Riley!" Derek said when he saw him. "We heard there was a party!"

Riley held his dog against his chest. She was yipping and slurping his neck and face and wiggling. Her big sweet ears stood up, and her tail swished madly. He sat down on the first bench he saw and let her down, holding her by her leash. She put her paws on his knees and rubbed her head on his thigh.

"Here, sit down with me, Bernie," he said. "And tell me what's going on." He stroked Sweetly.

"Auntie Margaret was all worried," Bernadette said. "So she said Derek should come see if you were okay. Uncle Richard said he shouldn't come by himself, and Derek said he wanted Trinh along, and Auntie Margaret said—oh, I don't remember anymore. Derek, what did your mother say? How come I got to come?"

"It sounds to me like Uncle Richard had a very good idea," Riley observed. Leave it to Richard to put a little sugar in Margaret's lemon juice. All to check up on him! What a silly woman.

What fun.

Derek was bent close to the woman's head, snipping carefully. He had taken at least a foot of hair off. "Just a minute," he said, hardly opening his mouth, and then he crooned to the woman, "Pretty, oh, you've got the nicest hair, you're going to look like Princess Di, I swear you are." Riley didn't think the woman could understand a word, but she got the drift of it. She was grinning happily.

Riley used the time to catch his breath. Then he broke

into a giant smile. "What a pleasure! What a surprise!" He grasped Bernadette's hand. "You look like an angel. I'm so glad to see you." Sweetly was now on his lap and calming down.

Bernadette beamed. "They gave me time off at the school. They said it was a special occasion. I told them, I never thought I'd get to go to Mexico. All I ever went to was Lourdes. We prayed I'd get smarter. I think I did." Bernadette was a cook's helper in an elementary school. "Mrs. Welch gave me this—" She pulled out a St. Christopher medal from her collar.

"It's very pretty."

Derek plumped and smoothed his client's hair. He whipped off the towel and shook it behind him. Nearby, several onlookers applauded. There were a couple of young women lined up for their turns. "You look beautiful!" they told the woman with the new haircut. She did look nice, though Riley wondered if she would mind when she looked in the mirror tonight and realized what she had done. The part that fell over her face would be an annoyance. Or would it? Maybe it would be a badge of quality. "A boy from Chicago cut my hair," she could say. "A gringo."

Derek sat the next girl down and told her to wait a moment. He went over to give his uncle a hug. "There's nobody to cut hair in town but a barber, and he won't do the women," he explained. "So Trinh and I figured, what have we got to do this afternoon? Isn't it fun? Are you surprised?" He laughed. "Of course, I'm not licensed yet, do you think anybody will check on that?"

"I'm faint with amazement. You picked the perfect day. But how did you find me?"

Derek put his hand to his brow to shield the sun and looked around the square. "The nicest woman knew where you were. We met her at the hotel."

"Don't say."

"Brenda?"

"Ah, Brenda."

"I heard my name!" Brenda called from behind Riley. She ran to him and kissed his cheek. "We're all coming over for the dance," she said. "Everyone's dying to see you. We thought you were long gone to Chicago, you naughty, self-ish, secretive devil, you."

"Everyone?"

"Joe. Renata. A couple you haven't met. And Les and Kitty. It's going to be so much fun!"

Riley didn't know what to say.

"I'm going to find a phone and call to see when they're coming," she said, and off she went.

"Got to get back to work," Derek said gaily. "Another surprise, huh?"

"Margaret told me about this," Riley said. "Hair, instead of liberal arts."

"And that's Trinh," Derek said. His friend stopped snip-ping and waved his scissors at Riley. "He's my very very best friend now." Something in his manner said, And that's only half of it.

Sweetly was panting in Riley's lap. "I think she's thirsty."

"Hang on," Derek said. He had a backpack on the ground near his feet. He dug in it and came up with a bicyclist's water bottle and a small plastic bowl. He poured water and held it out for Sweetly, who lapped it up, then settled back contentedly.

"Can't you take a break?" Riley asked. "I'll take you to the cantina. We'll have a beer to celebrate."

"We couldn't," Derek demurred. "Look how we'd disap-point them." He swept his arm to show the scope of his gen-erosity. There were nearly a dozen women waiting.

"I can go," Bernadette said.

Riley took her arm. "I'm just so pleased to see you," he said.

Derek took the dog. "She is ready for a nap, don't you think?" he said. He laid her down under the bench in the cool shade, and after a bit of self-arranging, she did indeed sigh and settle.

"I got a raise," Bernadette told Riley as they crossed the plaza and the street to the little sod-floored cantina. He told her he was delighted to hear it. Inside the cantina, it was dark and cool and crowded, so early in the day. He bought bottles of Corona and limes and led her back outside. They leaned against the wall to drink. Bernadette watched him rub the lime along the rim of the bottle, then carefully mimicked him. He was careful to take a small sip, as did she.

They looked around when they heard some shouts and shrill whistles. "Look at the car," Bernadette said. It had to be the reason for the excitement. It was a low-rider, a shell-pink Chevrolet with a long white stripe that curled on the back fenders. It had a Texas plate. The man driving leaned out of the window and waved vigorously as he drove past the plaza on the one open street.

"Is he someone important?" Bernadette asked.

Riley answered, "I'm sure he is to someone, honey."

When he saw that Bernadette had drunk half the beer, he suggested they take a walk. "I'll show you a little of the village."

"There you are!" Brenda had found them. She took his other arm. "Everybody's coming at six. Joe needed a good nap first. Did you know they dance before dark? I guess they want to see everyone. I want a dance, Riley. And Bernadette—there'll be lots of boys wanting to dance with her."

Riley accepted his fate. "Come on, girls," he said. "Let's see what there is to see." He squeezed Bernadette's arm.

"This is the village where your mother and I came on our honeymoon. We liked it very much. That's why I came back."

"That's so romantic," Brenda said, but there was an edge of worldly weariness to it.

Along the streets they found the village preparing for the afternoon and evening's festivities. Girls were scrubbing younger children in tubs outside their doors. Others were brushing and braiding hair. Everywhere, radios blared. A surprising number of villagers called out, "Good afternoon, Señor Riley," and he felt proud, as if he had accomplished something simply by becoming familiar. He answered them warmly, and Brenda, too, spoke cordially. It was like wending their way through a snaky long reception line.

"They know you!" Bernadette said. "I don't know what they said, but I understood your name."

He explained that they had greeted him. "They're very polite," he said. "They're really very nice." He taught her how to say "Good evening." She did so, many times, which pleased the villagers, who liked their greetings and appreciated even humble effort with their language.

He took the women to the chapel. Since last night, it had been transformed. Outside, banners were hung over the doors, saying, "OUR LADY," and "SPEAK HER PRAISE," and "HOLY HOLY." Inside, the chapel was decorated with garlands of fronds, and branches stuck with paper flowers—pink, blue, purple, yellow, and scarlet. Incense was burning in a dozen spots in the room, and the benches had been hung with crepe paper at the bottom.

"It's so much prettier than Sacred Heart," Bernadette said. "Couldn't we put paper flowers up at home?"

"I bet they do sometimes," Riley said. "We just don't go at the right time."

From there he took them up the street toward the Arispe house. As he approached it, he saw that the pink Chevrolet was parked there, effectively blocking the street. They stood across from the house. "I have friends who live there," he said. He looked at Brenda, who didn't react. "But I suppose they're busy now." The door was thrown open and they could see what seemed to be a throng of people inside. There was a lot of noise coming from the house—shouts and laughter and music. He couldn't catch a glimpse of Divina or Consolata. His heart pinched at their absence.

"Come on," he said, "I'll show you where I've been staying."

Both women raved when they saw Pete's house. He saw the gardens freshly again through their eyes, the bubbling birdbath, and the gargoyles above the door. He suggested they sit in the courtyard a little while, before the dance. He suggested they might freshen up, and showed them the bathroom by his room.

In the courtyard, waiting for them, he could only wonder at the events of the day. When they came back, he said, "Did you call Margaret to let her know you're safely here?" but Bernadette couldn't remember whether Derek had or not.

"Pete's got a phone now, we really ought to call," he said. He wasn't eager to talk to Margaret, but he could imagine she hadn't left the phone all day.

Brenda had found a comfortable chair, a long chaise-style made of latticed leather. "You go on, I'm very happy here," she told them.

Margaret answered on the first ring. He told her the kids had found him, all right. "You should have told me they were coming," he said. "I'd have arranged rooms and all."

"Now how was I going to do that?" she demanded. "Since you wouldn't answer my calls? How was I to know you weren't dead and buried? Or, at the very least, languishing with one of those tropical diseases?"

"Oh, Margie," he said. "Everything is so, so fine here. You should have come, too."

"Now, Tommy," she said. She sounded pleased. "When are you coming home? We do all miss you ever so much, you know."

"Very soon," he said. "You'll be surprised when you see me, I've gotten a tan."

"Don't let that Trinh boy cut your hair," she warned. "He's a devil with the scissors."

"I only just met him," he said. "He's a striking and interesting young man."

"Talk to Derek," Margaret pleaded. "I think this is all just a phase, don't you?"

"I don't even know what you're talking about," he replied.

"I'm talking about that boy. I'm talking about them."

"Here's Bernadette, say hello," he said quickly, and gave his stepdaughter the phone.

He sure wasn't going to say anything to Derek. Let Derek volunteer whatever he wanted him to know.

As it turned out, it wasn't necessary for anybody to say anything. Some things are as obvious as sunup. By the time Riley and Bernadette and Brenda got back to the plaza, the festivities had begun, the haircutting was over, and Derek and Trinh were strolling around, arm in arm, so obviously in love they might have been wearing a banner proclaiming it. Gringo butterflies, the villagers would say, but, being gringos, the boys were already from another planet. It was nothing to the village. And it was, to his own surprise, nothing to worry about for Riley, either.

Who would I be to criticize an unconventional love? he

thought, though he knew, with a twinge, that it would take some getting used to.

"Uncle Riley," Derek said. He had cornered him while Trinh tried his luck in the makeshift "bull ring," making passes with a banana frond at a baby goat. The boys in the ring were laughing and chasing them both—Trinh and the goat—and so were chickens and a small pig. Onlookers were enjoying the spectacle. They threw coins in and the little boys scrambled to collect them.

"I need to talk to you," Derek said.

"I don't think it's necessary at all," Riley said. "I'm sure you've received enough advice from your mother."

"Oh, Uncle Riley, I don't want advice. I want a lease!"

"You do?"

"The thrift store has vacated the premises. You have that nice space right next door to you. Trinh and I want to open a salon."

"A salon."

"He's fully licensed, and it won't be long for me. His sister does manicures and pedicures, and they both have a clientele that will follow them from where they are now. We'd be such good renters, honest, and we'd be great neighbors."

"I have to say I'm surprised."

"We have to get a little loan for equipment, and then we'd be up and running—"

"And that's me, too?"

"I think Dad would put up most of it. We need the space from you."

Riley couldn't help smiling hugely. "I go out of town and look at how much happens."

"I'm so happy!" Derek exclaimed. "I hated school. Then I met Trinh at a jam session—" Derek played jazz sax, fairly well. He raised his hands, palms up. What was there to say about something so obvious?

"Of course we'll work something out. But there is one thing. You'll need to find your own place to live, when you can afford it."

"I practically live with Trinh already. I'm just at your place to mind the dogs."

"I appreciate that."

"Is someone else moving in?"

"That part is my surprise. I'm not ready to tell you yet."

"Uncle Riley!"

"Uncle Riley wants to buy a garland for Bernadette," Riley said, pointing at a vendor's stand piled high with strung flowers.

"You'll love him, too," Derek said. He was looking across at Trinh and beaming. "Isn't life full of surprises?"

"Isn't it?" Riley said. "Isn't it just."

Fiesta

PEOPLE WERE WANDERING AROUND IN CLUSTERS. Mostly they looked solemn. Only the children, dressed up and lively, were really merry. Everyone was on the move but there wasn't any way to tell where it was they meant to go. Many were in masks with straw hats and bleached cowhair, dyed chicken feathers, and so on. Decorations seemed to be made of anything—bread dough, flowers and fruits, cut paper. Buses had come in from other villages, and the whole plaza was thronged. The smells of barbecued meat and chiles were everywhere.

They saw a woman wearing a headdress made of snake-skins and dead lizards. And tourists from Guadalajara, dressed in expensive clothes, looking amused. Others, in shorts and T-shirts, were gringos. Riley saw one of them ask the woman with the lizard hat if he could take her picture. She bent, raised her hands, fingers out, and hissed him away.

At one of the stands, Riley bought everyone one of the favorite village drinks, a potent concoction of tequila, rum, egg, and almond milk. He included several villagers whom he knew by sight, and who looked eager for a round. Bernadette tasted hers and made a face. The villagers laughed and teased her, with good spirits, and she enjoyed the fuss far more than the drink. The boys whooped and hollered and had a second shot. The mayor, Don Genaro, came over, and Riley introduced everyone. By then, Brenda's Joe had joined them, and another couple from the Posada Celestial. Don Genaro was with a young man. He introduced him as his son, Sebastian, who had come over from Guadalajara for the occasion. Sebastian was tall and slim, with a beautiful face and stunning hazel eyes. It was the first time Riley had noticed that Genaro, too, had those extraordinary eyes, which took on different colors with the changes in light.

Riley looked all over as they walked, hoping to see Divina. He saw Yzelda and asked her if she knew where Divina was. Yzelda said, "She's here, who knows where?" and asked Riley if he'd dance with her when the music started. He said he would be delighted.

A small orchestra set up at one end of the plaza and began to play. Dancing began immediately. True to his word, Riley spotted Yzelda and asked her to dance. She was wearing a nice strawberry-colored dress with a full skirt. After he danced with her, a village boy appeared eagerly and twirled away with her. She looked back to grin at Riley; he'd been her gringo bait. He waved.

He danced with Brenda, and her friend, and of course with Bernadette. Trinh danced with Bernadette, too, and so did Joe Flaxman. The music stopped, there was a moment of quiet, then it started again, with an excited flourish.

A parade had begun. There were several pickups, heavily decorated with colored paper and flowers, and numerous girls waving and giggling from the back. The princess—no surprise, it was Teresita—was on her lawn chair throne, waving her wand and blowing kisses.

The band stopped playing again. A hush fell over the crowd. The statue of the Virgin, decorated with a cloth dress and flowers, was propped in the back of the baker's truck. A young man crouched behind it, holding the base. The truck slowly cruised around the plaza, then turned up to the chapel. The priest walked behind the truck. Behind him, a procession of villagers fell into line, carrying long lit candles. Among the adults, there were little boys in surplices, and girls in white dresses. They followed the truck to the chapel, and went inside after the men carrying the statue.

The music began to play again on the square, louder and livelier than before.

Riley saw the pink Chevrolet. It passed where he was standing. Inside he saw Divina in the back seat. She leaned out the side window, smiling and waving. She was wearing something bright blue. She saw him, waved, and was gone. He hadn't even noticed who else was in the car, the car with the Texas plates.

Then he saw Consolata crossing the plaza in his direction. He almost ran to greet her.

She looked nice in a red skirt and blouse. She was wearing a rope of flowers around her neck. A spirited song was ending. He waited to see that it was followed by something more tempered. "Will you dance with me?" he asked. He put out his hand, and she took it. He led her onto the plaza stones. The music was nicely mellow, and the dance went smoothly.

"You are very pretty tonight," he said.

"My son Ruben came home," she told him.

"Then you are especially happy."

"He brought his wife and babies."

"In his pink car!" Riley realized.

"Yes. And a beautiful dress for Divina."

"I saw her in the car. All day I've waited to see her."

"And your friends—"

"My nephew, my stepdaughter, even my dog!" he said. They had taken Sweetly up to Pete's, where, Riley hoped, she was sleeping cozily.

The song ended. Riley stood beside Consolata. "I'm so happy for you, that your son has come."

"He is in night school in Austin," she said proudly. "He is studying computers."

"He must be smart and ambitious."

At that moment, Riley saw Divina dancing with Eusebio. She was radiant in a brilliant blue satin prom dress, her hair caught up in a net of blue and white ribbons. Riley flushed with anxiety. She looked so happy. Eusebio looked happy. What did it mean? He tried to think how to pose a question to Consolata.

He didn't have time. Don Genaro crossed briskly to them as the orchestra began to play again. "Excuse me," he said to Riley, and then he gave a small bow to Consolata and said, "May I have this dance, Consolata Arispe?" Several people noticed and watched as they began to dance. Riley watched, too. He could see that it was something special. A ripple of whispers passed through the crowd, and heads turned. Don Genaro, dancing with Consolata Arispe.

Sebastian, Genaro's son, approached Riley. He dipped his head briskly in greeting, then waited beside Riley as the music played. Bernadette had slipped up alongside Riley, too. He took her hand. She was delighted, he saw, with the festivities, and she was doing very well with it all. Someone had given her a candle. It was no longer lit, but she held it in her fist. "We'll light it later," he told her. "It's blessed, you know."

Don Genaro walked to his son, gently guiding Consolata. "Sebastian," he said, "I want you to meet my dear friend Señora Consolata Arispe."

Divina hurried to her mother's side. She was quite close to Riley, but hadn't looked at him directly. She took her mother's hand. At this moment, Riley realized, he was merely background to some other drama being played out tonight.

"And this is her daughter, Señorita Divina Arispe," Don Genaro said.

The young man looked stunned. So did Divina. Riley saw why immediately. They looked so much alike, anyone could see it. The eyes, the planes of their faces. Divina was the first to look away. Sebastian looked at his father, who pretended not to see.

Consolata had no particular expression. A faint smile, perhaps. Genaro looked simply determined.

"Enchanted," Sebastian said quietly.

Divina dipped her head. Consolata smiled. "So you are Don Genaro's fine son," she said. "Of whom I have heard so much." Now she looked at Genaro. She was a picture of dignity.

There was a small crowd around them now. Villagers watching in silence. Sebastian hid his private thoughts behind the face and manners of a poised, polite young man.

Riley stepped forward. "Divina," he said, "the music is beginning again. Please, will you dance with me?"

Now she directed her attention to him. She was more beautiful than he had ever seen her. The sun was setting, and the gold and red light made copper shadows and amber highlights on her face. In the Texas dress her brother had brought her, her shoulders were shockingly bare. She moved into his arms.

"Divina," he said. Over her shoulder he saw Derek and Trinh standing close by with Bernadette, watching him. "I missed you all day. There are so many things to say." He'd made a silly rhyme, but she didn't seem to notice.

"First the dance, Tomás," she said. She wanted everyone to see, Riley thought. Oh yes. He danced, and they wound their way around her mother and Don Genaro. It seemed a whole village of dancers. He was intoxicated with the music and with Divina's closeness. He danced. He tried to imagine they were cast in a movie from the forties. He made daring turns, then pulled her to him. On one of their turns, he saw Pete and a petite blond woman, and he lifted a hand to wave. Pete was smiling so big his smile seemed to take up half his face. Riley saw Eusebio standing alone, and his heart went out to him, but he turned and led Divina away. He saw the Americans from the hotel, staring at him. He couldn't tell what they were thinking; he only knew he was conspicuous.

"Divina," he said, and drew his focus in, away from everyone else, all those people who didn't matter.

The music stopped. There were people all around, watching. Some of the Americans applauded. Were they applauding the orchestra? Were they applauding him? Was it approval? Mockery?

His head was spinning.

"Divina," he said.

She clasped his hand and led him from the plaza. He glanced back to see that Bernadette was laughing, standing with Derek and others from the hotel. He walked quickly to keep up with Divina.

"Where are we going?" he asked.

"First, the chapel," she said. They entered and found it ablaze with the light from candles, hundreds of them set in clusters in glasses and jars and pots all over the chapel. There were a dozen women praying the rosary. Riley and Divina sat on a bench in the back, holding hands.

"Let's go to the Great House," she said. "I want to see Charlotte."

They reached the house. It was very quiet there. The

sounds from the plaza were now muted by the distance.

They stood in shadows. It was, suddenly, dark.

She touched his cheek with her long cool fingers.

"Divina."

Her face was turned up to his. He bent to her so slowly. His whole life was changing in a moment. He bent to kiss her, and she put her arms around his neck.

"Divina," he said. He yearned to touch her everywhere.

"Do you like my dress?" she whispered.

"Yes. And your hair."

"And the dance?"

"I loved the dance," he said.

"And me, Tomás?"

"I love you, Divina." It wasn't hard to say at all! His lungs filled, his chest swelled. "I love you!"

There was a pause when she said nothing. Long enough for the fear to rise to his head and pound in his temples. Long enough for him to imagine her kind refusal, the terrible moments of embarrassment, the long stretch of regret.

"Oh, Divina," he said, his voice thick with sorrow.

"I love you, too, Tomás," she said, almost matter-of-factly, as if she had said, *Didn't you know? Well, there, it's settled.*

He was nearly delirious with relief. "Could you leave Tecatitlán? Could you—Divina, would you marry me? Come live with me in Chicago?"

She threw her arms into the air. "Yes, as soon as we can. I don't want to wait. I've been waiting so long." She slid her arms around him. "I want to go to Chicago. I want to see your house." She pulled back. "What does it look like, Tomás? Your house?"

"It's two stories, with a big white porch where you can sit and speak to your neighbors as they pass. It's a sturdy house, built of brick. Inside, the walls are white and clean. The windows are tall. The floors are parquet."

"What is parquet?"

"It is wood, laid in a design. It was once very popular, when the house was built. It's pretty. The floors shine."

"I want to tell Charlotte," she said.

They found Charlotte on her veranda. She looked up as they came to her. She looked over the canvas that was propped on the easel in front of her. Her hair was caught back in chunks with long clips. She looked exhausted. Her blouse looked as if she had flung it on; it was unbuttoned over her T-shirt. When she saw them, she said, "Come around and see this."

The girl in the portrait was white and gold and copper and flesh.

Divina gasped. "Is it me?" Riley squeezed her hand.

He said, "It's wonderful, Charlotte." Then he saw that she had been crying.

"I won't give it to you," she said.

He shook his head. "It's yours, of course."

"And I'll show it."

"It's beautiful."

Divina knelt to lay her head in Charlotte's lap. "I didn't know it would be like that," she said.

"Nor did I," Charlotte said. "I thought it was an exercise." She pushed her hair back off her face. "Give me a minute. I'll wash and change, and we'll go see the fireworks together." Divina and Riley stood silently, admiring the painting, while they waited. When Charlotte emerged, she pointed to Divina's shoes. They were black with silvery straps and a low heel. Not village shoes. "I gave her the shoes when I saw the dress this afternoon. I told her the shoes had special powers. What are godmothers good for, if not for shoes that make a man stumble?"

"I knew she was joking," Divina said.

"I told her she had to let me see you with her in the

dress—and shoes, of course—or they would lose the magic."

Divina said to Riley, "She's kidding us," but she didn't sound entirely sure.

"Something did make magic," Riley said magnanimously. It wasn't out of the question that Charlotte had had something to do with the run of things. He felt as if he had been riding along a road following signs put up by someone just ahead of him. He had not so much earned his joy as accepted it.

"Charlotte the fairy godmother," he suggested.

"All the powers I have," she said, "are the powers of suggestion."

He understood why Divina had insisted they see Charlotte. She had become a woman here, in this studio.

"Look," he might have told her—and might tell her someday yet. "The world outside your village is full of wonder and terror, and full of every kind of surprise. So many would never dare venture out. But you were born of courage and fed hope and you are like the you in the portrait, ripe with the promise of your dreams. I will buy the tickets. I will take you to my house. But my life is in your hands. The painting promises me that much: The sleeping girl will waken. And if she is my wife, she'll tell me what I need to know to enter her dream. She'll pass to me some part of her magic. I'll be forever under her spell."

He could never say those things. But he could show her.

There were false starts. Sputters and fizzles, then the crackle and zing of the small firecrackers. Riley wasn't prepared for the spectacle of the great wheeled fireworks structure that came up the street. It was like an ancient, holy edifice. The crowd parted, stepped back, grew quiet. Several men were working with the structure. There were shouts and a curse or two, then long torches held to places on the limbs of it. For a moment, Riley feared some terrible error would be made. Someone would be hurt. But the wheel was at the intersection at one corner of the plaza, and there was a lot of room around it. As it began to sputter, then to shoot rockets and long spires of light into the air, onlookers stepped back even more. The entire thing burst into light. A long piece fell into the street like something live, jumping and crackling before it fell still. Babies commenced bawling.

Bernadette had found him. He put his arm across her and pulled her close. On the other side of him, Divina crackled in her satin gown.

The country buses were already turning their motors, ready to take their tired passengers home. At the liquor stands, some men lined up to drink seriously. They would spend the night in the street, then would cry out toward morning to find themselves here again.

Brenda and Joe found them. "We'll take the kids home," Joe said. He patted Riley's shoulder. "What a night. No Fourth of July, of course, but a great big wonderful amateur operation, nevertheless, wouldn't you say?"

Riley shook hands and hugged his family. Consolata and Don Genaro and his son came along, too. Then Ruben, Consolata's son, came. He was dark and handsome, and quite as poised as Don Genaro's son. He said his wife and children had gone to the house. Riley wondered how they would all sleep. Then he remembered his night in Mary of Tears, and knew there was always space for family.

"Come, we'll walk home," Ruben said. He took Divina's hand.

Genaro said, "I'll walk with Consolata."

"But we have something to tell you," Riley said. He was about to be abandoned.

Divina said, "Mama already knows."

"Tomorrow we will make plans," Genaro said. It seemed an odd thing for him to say.

"But—" Riley had expected Divina to be thrilled, to want all the village to know. He had thought of it as a rescue. *But it's me who is saved,* he thought. *The lucky man chosen to be the hero.*

Everything could wait until morning. He said his good-byes, with much handshaking and many embraces. He watched them all walk away. Divina smug, with her brother's arm around her waist. Genaro's proud stride beside Consolata.

He looked around. The square was emptying rapidly. The orchestra was packing up. He watched a truck back up by the fireworks wheel, and two men jump down to throw scraps in the back.

He looked around for Charlotte, but didn't see her. In the end, he made his way back to Pete's alone. He hoped he wouldn't disturb Pete and Cindy, but when he came in, he found them in the garden. A Nat King Cole song was playing. He said good night and left them; he could hear their happy voices as he went to his room. He found Sweetly asleep on his bed, burrowed down in the pillows. He went to bed in his clothes. The dog, not really waking, curled up beside him. He remembered the night he'd brought her home, the night he fell in love with Eva. *It was nothing like this,* he thought. *I loved, and now I love again.* He had gone from one country to another. At the border, everything had changed.

His anxiety was gone. In its place was a still joy, the joy one feels when things fall into place. He wasn't sure what came next; Consolata would know. Charlotte. Divina. The women would know. They would tell him what to do. He didn't mind at all.

A
Wedding

Don Genaro was having a very busy day. A clerk woke him not much past dawn to say that a circus was parking itself in the village, and planning a performance that very night. They needed electricity, there were permits and vendors' licenses for the day. The TV satellite people were due with his dish sometime after noon, and there was the matter of a wedding.

Riley would never have been able to manage it without Genaro. It wasn't enough that the priest gave his blessing, waived the banns, and suggested a five-minute service after the civil one. They could do something more in Chicago, with Riley's family, in Sacred Heart Church. But it took time to get a license in Mexico. It took time to fill out forms.

Don Genaro met them at the city hall. He'd arranged for the retired judge to get out of bed for the day, and he'd laid a few pesos in the court recorder's palm to speed up the paperwork. There was a lawyer from Lago, because the judge said it was necessary, but when it was all over, nobody knew what he'd done to earn his three hundred American dollars.

The lawyer was waiting in the street in front of the hall. He was a paunchy, pompous fellow in a shiny suit, mopping his face with a handkerchief and huffing about the way gringos wanted things to move so fast. He was wearing a ring with a canary diamond the size of an eyeball. "We've got it!" he said numerous times. "But it won't be easy!" Divina, in her white skirt and blouse, the one with the birds at the bodice, came along with Charlotte, and Riley was accompanied by his nephew. The lawyer reminded them that they'd need residents as witnesses, so they all stood in the street to decide who that should be. There was Genaro, of course. Imelda would love to place her X on some official document. Yzelda's mother. They'd find a fourth in the course of the day.

It was bound to take a while. They all trooped upstairs to the recorder's cubbyhole. She said she'd take them one at a time, insisted on it. Why not start with Divina? Charlotte stayed with her, and the others went off to the cantina on the square.

"It'll be a while," the clerk said. They all heard the first questions: parents' names, grandparents' names; there'd be a family tree before she was done.

Genaro went away to check on the circus. Riley got the cantina owner to find more chairs from his neighbors. By then Trinh and Bernadette had shown up. Trinh was carrying Sweetly in his backpack. Bernadette had a deck of children's cards in her bag, some sort of Go Fish. Riley told her to deal.

Divina arrived just as Pete and Cindy stopped by to say they were going to Mazamitla for a couple of days. "The house is yours," they told Riley and Divina. "With our blessings." They were as dewy-eyed as newlyweds themselves. Cindy couldn't keep from telling them, "We've put bread and chocolate in your room." She glanced at Pete fondly. "It's customary, isn't it?"

"Day after tomorrow we're going home," Divina said airily. "Will we see you before then?"

"I'm going back that evening, too," Cindy said. "Maybe we could all ride over." They talked about schedules and decided to work it out that morning of the flights. Divina was cool and efficient, like a seasoned traveler. She and Riley were going to be frequent flyers, after all.

Every once in a while a villager who'd heard about the wedding stuck his or her head in to give good wishes. Most didn't turn down the offer of a drink. The cantina owner had already sent for his grandson and a neighbor boy to help.

After a while a little boy came looking for Riley. "She can't do it if you don't hurry up," he'd been told to say.

Riley panicked. "Oh, God!" he said, and jumped up, upsetting the table and the splay of cards.

"Do what?" Bernadette wanted to know.

Riley ran over to the hall. Derek and Bernadette followed. Trinh stayed behind with the dog. Charlotte was coming downstairs as they went up. "You're going to love this," she said dryly. She stopped Riley and said, "Stay really calm, stay really firm, and keep your sense of humor."

Riley thought she might be kidding. It wasn't long before he saw she'd given him good advice.

He had to name a lot of relatives. He had to explain why he didn't have his birth certificate with him. He did have a passport, one he'd never used before; he'd gotten it when they first began talking about travel abroad, but the recorder's drill was, birth certificate, and Riley had to explain about the passport several times. There were important papers to be used with immigration at the other end.

The lawyer wandered in and out, examined these, and pronounced them done, like pie crust.

Riley swallowed hard and told himself they'd be man and wife, somehow he'd work it out. When the clerk shook her head, declaring some item a hopeless obstacle, he said, "Let's see what I can do," and managed, every time, to fill in another blank. The lawyer came and went; several times he leaned over to speak softly to the clerk, who nodded, sometimes yes, sometimes no. He brought cold drinks for her. He gave her a crisp, important-looking envelope. She promptly lifted her rear end, put it on the chair, and sat back down. Her ample bottom covered all evidence of bribery.

The clerk suggested they all leave and come back after lunch.

Lunch. Riley went to the cantina and sent the owner out to find food for them. He came back and said his cousin's daughter would make lunch. It was nearly two hours before it came. It didn't matter; the weary clerk had gone home for a nap.

Meanwhile, a few villagers came and went, and they met a pleasant fellow from Guadalajara who peeked in to see what the commotion was all about. Federico Rivera, the Arab, he said. He was full of explanations, and thrilled to be crashing a wedding. "I should be out on a site," he said, "but how can I leave yet?"

"Not exactly a wedding," Riley said, though what else was it? Divina had gone with Charlotte to look at a piece of luggage Charlotte was giving away.

"Why is your name Arab?" Bernadette asked. She was always utterly straightforward.

"It's a nickname," Federico said. "My father emigrated from Kuwait. He was a cotton buyer for my mother's family. Then we had cattle, but we lost everything in a volcano eruption. By then I was old enough for my own business. I started over in construction." There was more—much more—but so much else was going on and being said, his monologue was more like a radio than conversation. He'd lost Bernadette's attention by the third family profession. She was dealing two hands, hoping for a game.

It took four people to bring all the lunch. There was a clay pot of frothy beans, enchiladas, stewed goat, plates of chiles and rice and tortillas. The schoolteacher looked in because he'd let the students out early—he couldn't compete with a circus—and he'd heard about the wedding. They made a place for him to eat. Father Bernal came in when the schoolteacher had his plate heaping, and, with a bit of a sigh, the teacher moved over and made room. The priest couldn't stay long. When he left, he shook hands with the teacher. They'd learned in such a short while that they shared a fondness for Cervantes, and promised one another they'd get together soon for a discussion.

Federico went on and on. He was in town on business. He'd bought some lots, and he was going to build bungalows for weekenders from Guadalajara. He would be hiring local labor, he said. "First thing I'll work on is a water main," he said. "I do things right."

Riley perked up when he heard that. He said to Federico, "I've got an idea, if you'd be interested. We'll talk later." By then Genaro had shown up again, and Riley got up to talk something over with him just outside the door. Then he introduced him to Federico, who needed to know the mayor, of course. The two of them had hardly begun to talk when someone popped in to say that Genaro's satellite dish had arrived. "I can't come right now," Genaro said. "Tell them to do it right." There was more to pay, he said; it wasn't that he didn't have some leverage.

Divina and Riley went over to the hall to check on the progress of their license. Genaro went with them. The clerk had been working all day on a noisy manual typewriter. Now she had transcribed the information onto long creamy documents they would take away, red seal and all.

"You'll need your witnesses," the clerk said. "I've sent someone for the judge."

The lawyer was around somewhere. Couldn't he sign?

"Is he from Tecatitlán?" the clerk asked. He was not.

Downstairs a farmer in a big straw hat was waiting for his turn at business with the clerk. Genaro impressed on him the importance of his presence at their wedding. All he had to do, he heard, was sign his name. Or X. He swelled with importance and enthusiasm, and with all the activity that followed, never did do his business that day.

Genaro sent a kid from the street to get the other witnesses. While they waited, Genaro ran to his place to check on the dish. He came back out of breath but happy. "We can all go to my place later," he announced. "I don't know what's on, but I've got sixty channels."

The judge lumbered in. By then Consolata had managed to arrive. It was so crowded in the hall, he suggested they go across to the plaza. There was room there for anyone and all. People came out of the bakery to join the crowd. Yzelda and her mother were there. The old friends of Tía Filomena had found their way. On the edge, Eusebio was watching. And just past him, so was a stranger with a mustache and a baseball cap, and shoes made of strips of old tires.

Nobody noticed when the stranger found Eusebio, shook his hand, then embraced him. They left together before the short ceremony had begun.

The contractor, Federico the Arab, was there, too. He stepped up to give Divina a little kiss on the cheek. Riley said, "Here's what I wanted you to see," and took him over to the dry fountain. "Wouldn't a village fountain be a pleasant draw for your weekenders?"

"Let me see what it'll take," Federico said. "I've got equipment over here next week." He wanted to buy everyone a drink when they were done. "And I mean everyone," he said. The wedding was a bonanza of public relations opportunities for him.

The judge said he was ready, but just then a parade of schoolchildren went by with tin drums and a big banner announcing the circus. The dog Sweetly, who'd hardly been noticed in her bundled bed on Trinh's back, barked furiously. Riley put her on her leash and let her prance around the square. He fed her dog food from a vinyl lunch bag Derek had brought, then he walked her off for some discreet business. Someone had brought the judge a beer.

At last they all assembled by the fountain. The judge proved to be romantic, once Genaro had explained it wasn't a shotgun ceremony. He led them in Spanish vows. Genaro and Yzelda stood by the bride and groom. In halting English, at the end, the judge said, "I now pronounce you the man and the wife." He smiled and showed off his gold front teeth.

Riley shook hands with the lawyer and the judge, who had other business, they lamented.

They sent a boy on ahead to let Father Bernal know they were coming. Then they trooped off to the chapel. Yzelda's mother ran across the square to pop in a tray of cookies and said she'd catch up.

There were masses of flowers in the chapel. Riley was stunned. He hadn't even thought of flowers, in all the rush. Divina, beside him, held her hands to her cheeks in amazement.

Consolata stood by Don Genaro, and squeezed his arm.

The priest said, "We are gathered here to honor the marriage of Divina Arispe and Thomas Riley. A few weeks ago, they were strangers. Now they look forward to a long and blessed marriage. Though none of us might have predicted this union, none of us should doubt it. God is greater than the sum of all our hopes." And with that, he blessed the couple, and the gathering, the village, and the sacrament of marriage.

Everybody went back to the cantina for shots of tequila, beer, and tacos. Federico insisted on paying. Derek had Divina's boom box by now, and a handful of tapes. He tried a little Vivaldi, but soon switched to the Grateful Dead.

It was such a good party, hardly anyone noticed when Divina and Riley slipped away. They weren't there when an ecstatic Yzelda ran in, pulling on the arm of Reymundo, he with the mustache and tire-tread shoes, and the long tales of water trucks and circus trains, and longings for home. They certainly didn't care that they missed the move to Genaro's, and back-to-back episodes of *I Love Lucy.*

Nobody saw Riley and Divina again until nightfall, when they appeared at the circus. Someone had told the ringmaster about the wedding. He called them forward when the camel was in the ring. The big animal knelt and laid its neck down on the sawdust. Riley climbed on, with Divina in front. As the animal lumbered to its feet, Riley pressed his knees against Divina's thighs. His hands held her waist. With the lights in their eyes, neither could see Eusebio on the side, dressed in his overalls that said CIRCUS OF STARS on the back, pulling on a rope as Reymundo instructed him; nor did they see Yzelda in the seat nearest Reymundo, waiting for the show to end, and their lives to begin. They didn't see Don Genaro and Consolata slip out the back of the tent, though the show had not ended.

Someone called out, "Long life and many babies!" and Riley waved.

A
Fountain Flows

I SIT ON THE VERANDA EARLY ONE MAY MORNING and watch the hummingbirds at my feeder. It is quite dry already, and I have instructed Nola to keep the tubes full while I am away. We have had a lot of dust and Nola is afraid of it. I have seen her going out to do her chores on the veranda with her scarf around her chin, pulled up to cover her mouth. Nothing I say convinces her that dust is a nuisance, not a menace.

There is a special day approaching, when the standing crosses in the village are laden with bread and carved melon rinds, and Father Luis blesses them. I thought about staying, but I have seen it before, and it is hot, and my mother is waiting. I would have gone a little sooner, but I was waiting to see the fountain flow. I promised Riley I would take photographs. I did so, but I also took my pad down and did a series of watercolor sketches, thinking that I'll frame the best and send it to them as a wedding present.

In my mail a few days ago I found a photograph of Divina. Her hair is cut in a sleek bob just above her shoulders. She is standing sideways on the porch, one hand on the rail as if for balance. She is exaggerating her slouch, to show the slight slope of her pregnancy, and has a dramatic, mysterious, slightly bored expression, straight out of *Vogue*. I took it that same evening to Consolata, who had another from the same batch. In Consolata's, she is smiling. Divina had written to say she wanted her mother to come at Christmas and stay through the birth.

"You must go," I said, though I didn't know how Consolata would manage everything. "Can you close the cafe?"

She seemed uncharacteristically shy. "I am teaching Yzelda and Reymundo the business," she said. "They will run it while I am gone, and then, later, another little cafe here in Tecatitlán."

"That's wonderful!" I had not realized she had prospered so.

"I have an investor, you know," she said. "We are constructing a building for me, next to the grocery, where the old pottery shop used to be."

Suddenly I understood. I clasped her hand. "Genaro," I said.

She nodded, smiling. "A grocer, after so long, is a bored man," she said. I was dying to ask if they would marry, but I suspected they would not. I thought Consolata had just about everything exactly as she wanted it.

When I told her I was leaving, she embraced me and called me *comadre*. There is no English equivalent. Friend, but more than friend. I hoped I was.

"I will be back," I said. "I'm going to help my mother with the motel this summer. And to show some of my work. I've done a lot of watercolors of the village. And some of my drawings of Divina, I think, are worthy." I was nervous as I said, "There is a painting, too. I have been meaning to ask you if you want to see it."

"Divina told me about it," she said. She shook her head. "It isn't necessary for me to see. I know her at every age. I have paintings in my head." I took this as a permission of sorts. Or an acceptance.

"You knew, didn't you?" I asked. "That night you came to me at my house, before Riley came to the village. You knew what would happen."

"Not when I came," she said. "Not until you helped me tell the story."

"Do you have any idea, Consolata, what it has meant to me to be your friend? To live here?"

"It has been a home to you?"

"I've never loved anyone the way Divina loves Riley. The way you love her. I loved my daughter, of course, but not with passion. Not until she died. But I've learned there are other ways to love. As I love your daughter. As I love friends. I hadn't known that friendship could be a passion, too. I'll be back."

"The gift for friendship is inside you, Charlotte, not inside the village. Tecatitlán is just a place."

"I don't understand."

"Come back, as Pete and Cindy will come back. As my Divina will come back. My Ruben. But you don't have to live here to love."

"Consolata, I don't even know if I love my own mother!"

"Then it's time you learned," she said. She sounded almost stern.

I called my mother to say I was leaving. Coming. I could hear gladness in her voice. "I've cleared out one of the rooms for you, as a studio," she said.

"Don't expect too much, Mom."

"There's a balcony. It looks out on the valley—ridges and ridges of trees and brush. You don't see a single road or house. I know you like your solitude."

"It will take me a week," I told her. "I'm not pushing it."

"I'll say," my mother said. I hadn't been home in over two years, and I hadn't stayed more than a week in the last fifteen years. There are all kinds of ways to start over.

Elias came as I was loading the Jeep. I had taken everything out of my room. He caught me at the door, and I saw that he was sad at the room's emptiness.

"Let's go look at the little house," he said. I hadn't been to the lot in a month. It was a piece of the judge's old cleared orchard, with a slice of a view of the lake, and a fine view of hills. Federico, the "Arab" from Guadalajara, was building a small house for Elias. For me, Elias said. We had all talked about the plans. It was to be open and airy, but I had suggested painting the inside walls a pale blue, to offset the fierceness of the light on white. And I had asked Elias not to overplant. I preferred a sparer garden, and room for vegetables, later.

"I don't know what I will be able to pay," I'd told him. We'd gone round and round about it. He wanted to give it to me; I wanted to buy it. I had no money, no real money. "And I'll be gone part of the year, anyway. You could rent it."

"There's a maid's suite. I'll get someone. Maybe Nola would like to live there instead of at home and look after it. It wouldn't take much time until you're back. Look, it's a good investment for me if you don't want it, but I'm not ready to accept that as a decision yet. Let's say you'll have it next winter. Federico promises it will be ready by then."

"Okay." I did want to return.

The walls and girders were in place, and the masons

were making the brick vaulting. There were at least a dozen laborers around the site, all of them bustling.

Elias wanted to show me the nice windows he had brought from Guadalajara. They were stored in a makeshift shed to the side of the construction. They would have real shutters, that opened and closed. And he was installing sliding latticed doors on the veranda, so that I could control the light, for painting.

I laughed nervously. "I'll tell you what I told my mother. Don't expect too much."

"You haven't been painting lately?"

"Some watercolors. Mostly, I've been writing. I've finished a solid draft of a new book. I'm ready for an agent to take a look at it. I'll send it to New York as soon as I get to Wimberly."

"So quickly. Or is it something you've been writing all along?"

"Not at all. It's a simple story, that's all. I never saw how simple, before. I thought the only way to simplify anything was to run from it."

"You've become very philosophical."

"I'm intoxicated by the idea that I might actually do something. Notice I didn't say 'meaningful.' I didn't claim I would cross any datelines. I'm just happy that I feel like working again. Miracles do happen."

"Oh, yes. I remember I had my doubts once upon a time."

I didn't understand what he meant, but he wouldn't say. He preferred to give me mysterious looks, then laugh.

We walked back slowly. We were going to have lunch at the Great House, and then I would follow him back to Guadalajara, where his mechanic would go over the Jeep before I headed, the next day, toward Monterrey, then Texas. I had protested everything, but it all made so much sense, and, truthfully, I was grateful.

"Could you wait a few minutes for lunch?" I asked as we approached the house. "I want to say goodbye to Luis."

"Of course," Elias said.

I found Luis in the courtyard. I sat on the bench beside him. I hadn't seen so much of him recently; neither of us, it seemed, was up till all hours in the night anymore.

"What do you make of it?" I asked him. "Being able to sleep?"

"It's the byproduct of a little firmer faith," he said, and laughed. "It's the troubled soul that wakes."

"I'm glad you're feeling better."

He held my hand between both of his. "I'm going to miss you," he said.

"I'll be back."

"So all the migrants say."

I laughed.

He let my hand go. "Thank you for the box of books." I had left it for him the day before.

"You're welcome. I'll bring more back with me." I got up.

"Wait for the surprise," he said.

I couldn't imagine what he meant, but at that very moment, a bell pealed above us.

Luis laughed and clapped his hands together.

"You've got a bell!" I said. "The chapel has a bell!"

It rang again, and then I heard someone shout: "God is love."

Elias, of course, and his forgotten promise. I was happy for the village. A fountain and a bell. Some children home, and others gone.

"See you," I said to Luis. I was almost in tears. Elias came out of the chapel, grinning from ear to ear, and we went to lunch.

*   *   *

Near the Texas border, I turned my thoughts to my little book. It had no ending.

Here's where I stopped: with Divina and Riley, who have a history now. The miraculous luck of it. The bell ringing behind me in the chapel at Tecatitlán. The doors that will slide on the terrace of the new house.

Riley's photograph of Eva is in a frame now, hung in the hall outside the room they are decorating as the nursery. He thinks of her less often now, and never speaks to her. She has ceased to be his wife, of course. He is grateful to her for the ways she made him a better man. As he is grateful to Consolata for her wisdom. But it is Divina who is now his present and his future. His fire in the field. His chance to see Egypt.

He lies beside her on the first hot night of May. She has kicked off the sheet in her sleep, but thrown one leg over his. He lies awake for a long while, watching the light on the wall when a car passes.

He thinks of himself as an agent of something that was meant to happen. He thinks of love as a sweetness and a goodness, and passion as a gift. He doesn't know when it was that he became a reflective man, or a brave one, and the funny thing is it was all so easy. That, he thinks, is the nature of a miracle.

He dreams of the Nile. He is on a barge with Divina. They are drifting into dawn. They come around a curve into view of an amethyst sky, and against it, the massive monuments he never thought he would see.

"Look," he says, jabbing a finger toward the sky, trembling. It is all he knows to say, pointing, pointing. "Look what lies ahead."

Acknowledgments

I want to express my thanks to the Oregon Institute of Letters and the Oregon Arts Council for helpful assistance;

and my gratitude to my friends who stoked the fire: Gil Dennis, Tod Davies, Janice Gabriel, and Paul Steinbroner;

to Richard Rodriguez for generously sharing a gem of information;

to Betty Marsh for more than twenty years of hospitality;

to Maureen Earl for the week in San Miguel;

to Joe Eckhardt for the birds;

to Linda Eckhardt for so much of the spice;

to Mary Economidy for all those bus rides around Jalisco;

to my writing soulmate Bonnie Comfort for the phone lifeline;

and of course to my editor, Diane Reverand;

and to my perfect agent and friend, Emma Sweeney.

For those who love to read of Mexican village life, beyond all the rich academic material available, I mention two wonderful books.

Mexican Village, by Josephina Niggli, first published in 1945, is simply a treasure. It has been reprinted by the University of New Mexico Press. It is a reminder of how delightful "old-fashioned" storytelling can be.

The second book, sadly, is out of print, but I found it through interlibrary loan, the greatest library service ever invented. It is *Village in the Sun,* by Dane Chandos, published by Putnam's in 1945. It is a memoir of a year in Ajijic, Jalisco, and is rich in description and affection for the people. It was invaluable to me.

© 1996 by Mary Economidy

SANDRA SCOFIELD was born and raised in West Texas. Her many literary awards include nominations for the Oregon Book Award, the National Book Award, and a fiction award from the American Academy of Arts and Letters. She has also received an NEA/USIA New American Writing Award and fellowships from the National Endowment for the Arts, the Oregon Institute of Letters, and the Oregon Arts Council. In 1992 she received an American Book Award. Scofield is the author of *Gringa*, *Beyond Deserving*, *Walking Dunes*, *More Than Allies*, and *Opal on Dry Ground*. She works at Bloomsbury Books in Ashland, Oregon.